NO SECOND WIND

A. B. GUTHRIE, JR.

No Second Wind

HOUGHTON MIFFLIN COMPANY BOSTON
1980

c. 2

M

Library of Congress Cataloging in Publication Data

Guthrie, Alfred Bertram, date
   No second wind.
   I.   Title.
PZ3.G95876No   [PS3513.U855N6]   813'.5'2   79-23119
ISBN 0-395-29069-4

Printed in the United States of America

S 10 9 8 7 6 5 4 3 2 1

JUN 2 3 '80

For Ferol and Marty,
those prized companions

NO SECOND WIND

"DEAD COWS," Sheriff Chick Charleston said. "Cows killed God knows how." He was looking, not at me, but at his desk and the papers arranged on it.

We were seated in his office, where the radiators wheezed and banged against the outside cold. It was barely warm enough in the room, barely warm enough wherever people worked or lived. The mercury that morning registered thirty-five below.

"I've read something about that," I answered.

He went on as if I had not spoken. "Genital and rectal areas removed, by knife or shears or maybe only coyotes. No blood in the body cavities, or so little of it as to stump the experts."

Still looking at the desk, he shook his head, and went silent.

I was about to go to work again as one of his deputies. My father had died suddenly at the end of the winter quarter of my senior year in college, and I had returned to Midbury for the funeral and decided to stay for a while, if only to help my mother adjust. She had objected, maintaining I should go back to school and get my degree, but the sheriff and I changed her mind, though not beyond lingering doubts.

Charleston continued. "No footprints, either. None around the carcasses. Not a bootmark. Not a paw print."

"Not surprising in weather like this," I said needlessly. He knew there was no snow on the ground and the Arctic cold had frozen the earth hard as stone.

He nodded. "Stories get made up, some maybe on the mark, some crazy. Blood cults. Sex cults. Midnight helicopters that can't be traced. UFOs. Tall men, pygmies, hooded in black." He shook his head. "Spook the citizens, and you get spooky reports."

He had paused in his itemization as if counting. Now he straightened, and his eyes lifted. "I get notices from all around, from other counties and other states, but so far we've been spared. At least I hope we have. But there's a little case coming up in city court in the morning. I want you to be there, asking questions. You'll be allowed to. I've seen to that. It's only a justice of the peace case, before old Joe Bolser."

I asked, "Who's on trial?"

"Ike Doolittle. Know him?"

I didn't.

"Little old man, another Gulley Jimson."

"I don't know him, either."

Charleston shook his head, his smile rueful. "Higher education, and you haven't read about Gulley."

There was nothing to say to that.

"Anyhow, here are the questions."

He named them for me.

The courtroom, if it could be called that, was Joe Bolser's office, at the opposite end of the courthouse from the sheriff's quarters and one floor up. A desk served as the judge's bench. It had a law book on it, which was meant, I supposed, to be evidence of the judge's credentials. Ranged in front of the desk were half a dozen wooden chairs besides one set at the side for witnesses. Farther back were ten or so folding chairs unfolded for spectators and auditors if any.

An overhead light was turned on and needed to be. The cold had plated the three windows with ice.

My old friend, Felix Underwood, the undertaker, was already seated up front when I arrived. He gave me a bare salute as if the coming proceedings were solemn as a funeral.

Pretty soon Silas Wade, city attorney, showed up and took a seat. We exchanged helloes. He was a young fellow, just out of law school and, like all beginning lawyers, in his mind was probably climbing the political ladder. I thought I could follow his vision. Lieutenant governor, maybe, attorney general, governor and then on to Washington. Who knew?

We waited for Joe Bolser, who came in presently, sat behind the desk and cleared his throat. We didn't stand up at his entrance. Justices of the peace didn't deserve that much respect. It was going far enough to address him as judge. He was an elderly, paunchy man whose clothes didn't fit, and he squirmed in his chair as if crotch-bound.

Satisfied as to crotch comfort, Bolser cleared his throat again and shuffled some papers he had brought with him. Among them was a legal pad on which he meant, I guessed, to take notes. Justice of the peace courts didn't bother much with records. Names, addresses, offenses, dispositions — they were about all.

The judge took a pen from his pocket and, pointing it at us, said, "Before the court is the case of Ike Doolittle. I see the

3

complainant is present." Looking at Wade, he asked, "Where is the defendant?"

The door opened as he spoke, and a bundle of a man walked in. "Just in time, your honor," the bundle said.

"Be seated."

Before he sat down, the bundle unbundled himself, removing a sheepskin coat that must have come from an Old Testament flock. Without it he became a little specimen, a spider of a man, with a beard that a musk ox would have envied. Box him up, I thought, and you could send him by parcel post, beard included.

"Are you ready?" Bolser asked Wade.

"Ready, your honor."

Doolittle didn't have an attorney, so Bolser asked, "Are you ready, Mr. Doolittle?"

"Ready as ever I'll be. If the court please, let the mills grind." His mouth hardly showed he was speaking. It was his beard that did.

"I call as witness Mr. Felix Underwood," Wade told the court.

Bolser told Underwood, "Come forward and be sworn."

Felix took the oath and sat down in the witness chair. He wore his solemn, funeral look.

"Now, Mr. Underwood," Wade said. "Tell the court in your own words just what happened. What is the basis of your complaint?"

"It isn't mine so much as my wife's," Felix said. I believed him. I knew Mrs. Underwood.

"But she isn't present to press charges," Wade said half as a question.

"No. No. I was elected." One hand came to his undertaker's face. "Live and let live is my motto."

Judge Bolser asked, "Do you wish to withdraw your complaint?"

"No, Joe — I mean your honor — I can't do that."

"All right, then. Proceed," Wade told him.

"It was just last week, in the morning, cold like it is now, maybe colder — who knows? — and I got up in my nightshirt to turn up the heat. And there he was, in the same room as the thermostat."

"Who was, Mr. Underwood?"

"Him there. Ike Doolittle."

"You knew him?"

"Not right at first. I thought it was a buck sheep, a big one, that had come in and laid down. Then I saw his whiskers. It couldn't be nobody but Ike."

"What was he doing?"

"Nothing, unless making more water."

The judge lifted a gray eyebrow and asked, "Water?"

"He had that sheepskin of his open, and there was a pond on our new carpet, or say a wet patch of maybe three yards altogether, and that carpet cost me twelve dollars a yard."

"That seems excessive," the judge interjected. "I don't mean the cost. I mean the wet spot." He looked at the little figure of Doolittle. "From him."

Felix forgot himself and said, "You wouldn't believe it. You never saw so much piss. Neither did I, never in all my born days, man or boy."

"In your business you ought to know," Bolser said. He wasn't exactly grinning. "The court takes your word for it."

Wade picked up the questioning, "How did he happen to be in your house?"

"You'll have to ask him."

"Did he break in?"

5

"Naw. Naw. I never lock the front door."

"What did you do after finding him?"

"I didn't go close, not in my bare feet. I called the sheriff's office, and Tad Frazier came and took him away, leaving the evidence, you might say."

"Is Tad Frazier a witness?" The question came from the bench.

"I didn't think his testimony necessary," Wade answered. "I can get him, though."

"Never mind. Is that all, Mr. Underwood?"

Felix looked first at Wade and then nodded.

The judge dismissed him, and Felix came and sat by my side.

"Mr. Doolittle, do you want to be heard?"

"Could I explain a little and then throw myself on the mercy of the court?"

Judge Bolser said, "Mercy?" and hitched at his pants and thought for a moment. "At least you can explain, though that puddle, if you made it, will be hard to jump."

"No jumps, your honor. Just a poor man's annals, short and simple."

I knew the reference and looked sharper at Doolittle. It was hard to believe he had read Gray's *Elegy*.

"Come forward then and be sworn."

Doolittle rose and stepped ahead. There was so little to him that his feet made hardly a sound. Age? I guessed fifty. He said, "I can't take the oath, your honor."

"Why not?" An edge had come into Bolser's voice. "Do you propose to lie?"

"No, sir. It's in the interest of truth that I can't take it."

"Explain to the court."

"Your honor would have me swear to tell the truth, the whole truth and nothing but the truth, so help me, God. It's the whole-truth part that stalls me."

"Go on."

"Not meaning any disrespect, but I ask you who knows the whole truth? About anything? About you? About me? About what we done or seen? It isn't everybody who sees the same thing when they look at it or think it. Even the Bible ain't always so sure of itself. The whole truth gets away from all of us, even the Book."

A point all right, and Doolittle went on, "Take the apple. It meant different to Eve than to Adam, and what was the truth of it?"

He paused, and his eyes went from one of us to the other, above the shag of beard.

Staring at him, I thought about his speech, that hybrid of classroom and street, of books and bars. Well, even those of us who knew better lapsed from the rules, out of accommodation, habit or indulgence.

Bolser shifted and tucked his shirt tighter under his belt. "Will you swear to tell the truth that lies within your knowledge, all of it, so help you, God." I gave him a plus mark.

"Sure. I do."

"Be seated, then."

Wade straightened his young shoulders as if making ready to sink the harpoon. "You have heard the previous testimony, Mr. Doolittle. Do you dispute it?"

The judge interrupted. "Just a minute. For the record, Mr. Wade, we need his full name and address."

Wade appeared flustered. To be corrected by a mere j.p.! "Your name?" he said without much wind behind it.

"Ike for Ichabod, A for Armstead, Doolittle for me, though it doesn't fit."

"Your permanent residence?"

Doolittle fluttered his hands. "Permanent? Now that's a word. Permanent like in a hairdo? Here today and gone tomorrow. Permanent?"

"All right. Where are you staying?"

"I'm bunking at the Jackson Hotel, long as I can afford it."

"So, Mr. Doolittle, what is your version? What is the truth for which you have such respect?" I wanted to twist that kid lawyer's neck. "Tell the court in your own words."

Judge Bolser looked at us and said softly, "Who else's, pray tell?" I was liking him better and better.

"You want the long of it or the short?"

Wade answered, "Only what's pertinent."

"Well, I was working for old man Dutton, him with the pretty granddaughter, and we come to a disagreement, and I was fired or I quit. Take your pick."

"A disagreement, huh? So the present case is not the only trouble you've been in?"

"God help me, no. Not by a long shot."

"Did you come to blows?"

"With him! That's crazy. He's older than you and me put together. I admit he's spry, though. I bet he can turn handsprings. That's what his mind's always doing. Handsprings. Only it falls on its ass a lot. Begging your pardon, your honor."

"The court has heard worse. Now let's get more order into this hearing. Where did this occur? Your pardon, Mr. Wade."

"At his ranch. You know, 'way up there north and west of town. Like I said, Dutton's 'way along in years and" — he put his hand to his temple and made a winding motion — "he

8

imagines things or forgets them, even if he does sign the checks. Age, it plays dirty tricks on a man."

Wade was recovered enough to ask, "What was the cause of the disagreement? Why did he fire you?"

"He thought I was sweet on his granddaughter."

"And were you?"

The whiskers moved, presumably to a smile. "I thank you, sir, for those kind words, but the answer is double no. Take off thirty years, though, and I would have had a bow in my neck."

"We have been pretty far afield," Wade said. "Now let's get down to cases. You quit or got fired and — "

"And came to town. It had been a long time between drinks, and I tried to make up for that dry spell."

"You mean you got drunk."

"That's a weak word for what I was. I must have tried to take a drink for each thirsty day, like an old fool."

"And then?" Wade asked.

Doolittle turned toward Bolser. "You know, your honor, a man never gets used to the years. Even at my age he thinks he can hell around like the kid he once was. Pitiful, ain't it?"

Wade repeated, "And then?"

"I think I remember getting out of the Bar Star. What I do remember is it was so cold an Eskimo would have cried. Then, between whiskey and age, I got lost on my way to the Jackson Hotel, where I had stashed my plunder."

"What else do you remember?"

"I was wandering around, desperate, late at night, and here came a door, and it wasn't locked, and the place was warm, and I just went in and lay down and passed out."

"And also passed water," the court put in.

"I'm mighty sorry about that if I done it, and I guess I did. I must have a tank inside me. But a man's got to face up to what he did, drunk or sober, so I've already paid some cleaning people to go to that house and do their best when it's convenient."

"Are there other questions?" Judge Bolser asked as Wade indicated he was through.

"Yes, sir, a few," I said.

"Just whom do you represent?" Wade wanted to know.

"Shut up, Wade," Bolser said.

"To go back," I said to Doolittle, "just what were you doing at the Dutton place?"

"Everything I had time to turn my hand to. It's kind of run down, you know, and that poor girl was trying to take care of maybe a hundred beef, feeding them and all, keeping the fences up, keeping the cows inside, doctoring the sick ones and all the time trying to ride herd on a dotty grandpa. I kind of took over the outside chores."

"Did you dispose of a dead cow?"

"A long-dead cow, but pretty well preserved on account of the cold. It was to windward of the house and would have made a stink, come warm weather."

Wade, trying to show what attorneys were for, interrupted. "I don't see what bearing — "

If he hoped for renewed recognition, he didn't get it. "This is a leeway court, Mr. Wade," the judge said. "The questions may continue."

"What did you do about that cow?" I asked.

"I telephoned a rendering outfit, but it was no go there, too cold for those boys, I guess."

"So?"

"There was an old team of horses on the place and not much else in the way of power, so I hooked the team to the cow and pulled her onto a stone boat as old as time, and then I hooked the team to the boat, and away I went."

"Went where?"

"To a downwind coulee where I left the carcass."

"Did you take special notice of the cow, the condition it was in?"

"The condition was dead."

Bolser winked at me, and I had to smile.

"I understand that," I went on. "What killed the cow? Were there any marks on it, marks like wounds? Anything?"

"Not that I noticed. You have to understand that cow was old. God knows how many years she had on her. She should have been culled six or ten years before. Finally she just lay down and died. That's what the girl told me. The old man backed her up when he could think of it."

"What about the udder? The genitals?"

"Gone."

My questions had stirred curiosity. I could see it in the eyes and the gathered attention.

"Gone?" I asked.

"Varmints, critters like wolves, they go for the soft parts first. So those fixin's weren't there."

"Could you distinguish between knife work and tooth work, between a cut and a bite?"

"That would depend. Not on that cow, though. Too long."

"You mentioned wolves. There are no wolves in this section as far as I know. Haven't been for a long time."

"That's what they say, though I might think different. Things go and things come. There's a season for everything, like the Bible says." His whiskers moved to a smile. "On that cow, though, it could have been coyotes. I'm not set on wolves."

I had come to the end of my questions, and Judge Bolser asked, "Anything else?" Not hearing anything, he inquired of Felix, "The court will go by your wishes, Mr. Underwood? Obviously this man is guilty."

Felix was a long time in answering. At last he muttered, "There's my wife." Abruptly he shrugged and straightened. "But hell, the man's made — What do you call it, Joe?"

"Restitution."

"Yeah. Restitution. Hired those cleaners and all. Made a clean breast of things." He sighed and said, maybe thinking of his own old misdemeanors, "It could have happened to anyone."

"I thank you, Mr. Underwood," Doolittle said, still in the witness chair. "You're right. It could have happened to anyone, but more likely to an old fool drunk." The beard moved wide as he spoke.

Bolser said, "Case dismissed."

◆◆◆ **2** ◆◆◆

IT WAS TWELVE-THIRTY when court adjourned, and, feeling pretty sure Sheriff Charleston would not be in his office, I walked, hunched in my down coat, to the Commercial Cafe. There were few people on the street and few cars. The people hurried and dodged into doorways, sending out steam-engine puffs.

The cafe was almost empty. The workingman's lunch hour in Midbury is from twelve to twelve-fifteen. I sat at the counter and ordered the special. It was short ribs, and they were greasy enough to lubricate a tractor. I picked over the bones for meat not too oily for a goose and ate a boiled potato and a couple of sad carrots. Then I scoured my throat with a cup of scalding coffee.

"Hello, Joe College," Blanche Burton said from the switchboard as I entered the sheriff's office. She was a buxom old girl, long widowed, and, like a lot of older women, was more than a little arch. Hopeful to the last, I thought. Our community took good care of its widows, if not often by marrying them, then by seeing they got jobs.

"Afternoon, Sis," I said to please her.

She sat at a sure-enough switchboard, beside which was a radio transmission and receiving set. Communication to cruise cars. A new dispensation for the county. Night-and-day service, with three women alternating shifts. Not like the old days when Jimmy Conner, sitting before a lone telephone and a couple of jacks, answered nearly all calls.

"He's in his office, Sheriff Charleston, I mean," she said as if I didn't know what she meant.

Charleston was worrying with papers on his desk when I entered. He looked up, his eyes inquiring. He waved toward a chair.

"Home free, it looks like," I told him. "Doolittle said the cow was long past her prime and should have been culled years ago. Natural death, according to him. He was backed up, so he said, by Dutton's granddaughter and old man Dutton himself."

"Mutilations?"

"The bag and private parts were gone, probably eaten out by predators. He seemed pretty sure about that. He mentioned wolves but then switched to coyotes."

Charleston looked at the window, not through it, because no one could see past the glaze of ice. The radiators kept banging. He said, "Hmm. We can be thankful then."

I asked, "Just who are the Duttons?"

"I know them to see them," he said. "In fact, I caught a glimpse of her in town today. Pretty girl. Both parents died, the father just a year or so ago. Left her with a poor ranch and the old gaffer. I guess they must do most of their trading at Petroleum. It's closer. Once in a while, just once in a while, they come here."

I could tell his mind wasn't on the subject. After a pause

14

he said, "There's another problem, Jase, or likely to be."

I waited.

"It's the newcomers, the hard-hat breed. You've seen their camp?"

"From a distance. I haven't been across the creek."

"Campers, trailers, mobile homes, the like of that, some new, mostly old. Miners, the men call themselves. They're strip miners, machine operators, truck drivers, and they're just waiting for the go-ahead."

"Who says go or not?"

"Right now environmental agencies. There's a hearing next week. One company, Energy Associates, has leases, some of it on land above Chuck Cleaver's place."

Charleston moved his head sadly. "They would leave a spoiled land."

Abruptly he shook himself and sat straighter. "There could be bad trouble ahead. These men don't know land or the love of the land. They just think jobs and coal. They're a strange breed to us. They don't mix in, and we don't want them to."

"We?" I asked.

"Most, if not all, of the locals. The ranchers. There's tension, Jase. It could snap. Some little thing, or big, could do it. That's what I'm afraid of. Dislike into violence. Mob action." He shook his head. "So I want you to mingle, make friends with the strangers if you can, promote good relations, show the law's not taking sides."

"When do I start?"

"Whenever. I'm putting you on the night shift. You better go home now."

It was dismissal, and I got up. As I went to the door he held me up with, "And Jase."

"Yes, sir."

15

"Find me another deputy, too."

Walking from the building, I was struck with the thought that he looked tired, that he had begun to grow old. But I would have backed him against any man I ever hoped to meet.

I set out for home on foot, refusing the use of a police car that Charleston had suggested I take. In this weather — I passed an outside thermometer that registered forty below — a car was a questionable asset unless you were within easy reach of an electrical outlet and had an engine heater under the hood. Most people had them, which didn't do any good unless plugged in. Unplugged, an engine stiffened fast. The courthouse had a rank of outside outlets which the sheriff and other officials used. At home we didn't have one. If a driver had business along the street or wanted to idle over a couple of drinks, he often left his engine running.

Halfway home and half frozen, I saw her. She was coming out of Bloom's Grocery carrying a sack of supplies.

It happens. I know it happens because it happened to me. She was *the* girl. I watched her taking the sack to a car. I saw how she moved. I saw her face, bright and alive and clean-lined on this cold and misshapen day. I stood there, thinking to help her with the sack, and didn't move. She drove away. I didn't notice the make or color of her car.

I went into the grocery, trying to saunter. Bloom wasn't busy. He stood at the cash register and asked, "Something for your mother, Jase?"

"I dodged in to get warm. How's business? That last customer of yours must be a stranger. Know who she is?"

"Uh-huh!" he answered. "Uh-huh!" His fat face was grinning. "How come the law is interested in her?"

"Just curious."

"Sure you are. Just curious. Sure. That girl is Miss Anita Dutton and too good for the likes of you. Too self-reliant, too. Too independent. She wouldn't even let me carry her stuff to her car."

He was still grinning when I thanked him and left.

Outside there sounded the hoarse snort and pound of an engine, magnified by the cold, and a truck with a cab high as a balcony came roaring. On the flatbed behind it crouched a big bulldozer. It had the appearance of a bulldog about it, ready to tackle a mountain. And behind it rolled a trailer with two people in it. It turned off to the right, toward the row of movable homes.

I walked on to the Bar Star, wanting to think, not to drink. There wasn't a customer in the place, and Bob Studebaker welcomed me as if I had come to forgive his sins.

"On the house, Jase," he said. "A hot one. Just the thing to thaw a frozen ass."

He took a teakettle that was fretting on a single burner, poured some hot water into a mug, added a little sugar and filled the cup with brandy.

"I'll have one myself," he said, as if on second thought. "Cheer me up. Sad days, these are, sad for Midbury and the county."

"How so?"

"These goddamn strangers. These grease-monkeys. These gear-shifters. These big-shovel shits. Not welcome here, and they know it. This started as a stockmen's saloon, and by God she stays that way. Stockmen, honest businessmen, professional people like you."

His face flushed, either from the brandy or outrage. "So they set up their own place. Hauled in an old house, and I

17

guess outfitted it and bought some booze. They ought to be put the run on. Once in a while one or two of those jokers drops in here. Well, hell, this is a public place and I serve 'em. Not that I want to and not that they get any change out of me when it comes to talk. Goddamn foreigners."

I said, "Think so?"

"Sure. They call their place the Chicken Shack, though that ain't the way I pronounce it. But they serve chickens all right — roosters and a couple of laying hens, if you get what I mean."

I nodded, getting it, and took a swallow of my drink.

"But, hell," he continued, "you didn't drop in to hear my gripes. What goes with you?"

"Ike Doolittle's trial, held this morning. I was there."

"I heard he had to show up before Bolser. What happened?"

"Case dismissed."

"That's good." Studebaker put down his cup and patted his paunch, which had grown a little year by year, though it didn't look burdensome yet. It would in time, I thought. All bartenders tended to get fat, but not from home cooking. "I had a notion to lay a charge against him myself. I'm glad I didn't. It was what you might call a passing fancy."

I said, "I'd like to hear it."

"It's a long story — "

"And calls for another hot one. I'll pay."

Studebaker went through his ritual of hot water, sugar and brandy, and set the cups on the counter. That done, he told me, "It was about a dog, the biggest goddamn dog you ever seen, name of Gunnar." He took a big swallow. "Six, maybe eight customers were here, drinking sociable, and I was behind the bar, all innocent-like, and then the door opened. That was last fall, I should say."

He paused, waiting for me to get the picture or to add some suspense to his report. "Like I said, the door opened, and in came little Ike Doolittle and that monster of a dog. Afterwards he said he knew a little German but got mixed up. Anyhow, he pointed at me, and I swear he said, 'Get him, Gunnar.' Jesus Christ!"

I waited, knowing he would go on after an appropriate silence.

"Gunnar got the message all right. With one jump he came clear over the bar, knocking a couple of customers off of their perches. One look was enough for me. He had that big mouth open, showing teeth like an alligator. I vaulted over to the customers' side, and here he came after me. So it was down the bar we went, jump and jump, and him on my ass all the way."

He shook his head. "A man like me now, he can't keep in shape. Three leaps, and I was done for."

He wanted me to ask a question, and I did. "So he got you?"

"I passed out on the floor, customers' side." He patted his belly again. "I ain't made for the high jump."

I said, "Go on. I'm listening."

He went on, slowing his words. "Now wouldn't you think one of my customers would have tried to help me? Wouldn't you now? All my friends and good pay, and I pass out a good share of drinks free. Didn't I have a right to expect help? Wouldn't someone have done something? Well, I'll tell you, not one son of a bitch did."

For the sake of emphasis he fell silent, then said, "It was the dog that brought me to."

"I'll bet."

"You got it wrong. He brought me to by lickin' my face."

"You expect me to believe that?"

19

"It's the truth. When I opened my eyes, there was that big tongue bathing me. You see, Jase, that dog won't chew on dead meat, so to speak. Lie down helpless, and his heart breaks."

"Some dog. Was it Doolittle's?"

"Hell, no. It belonged to a fat German couple who was touring the U.S. Well, not exactly fat, but what you would call plump. Comes from eating all that damn sausage. Doolittle does know a little German, and the Germans spoke some American. So they got friendly, and Doolittle saw they was tired after a long drive and offered to walk the dog while they ate. It was then he decided to call on me. All the same, I got nothing against him. Turns out he done me a favor."

"Some favor. Scaring you half to death."

"That Gunnar's a good dog. Don't attack unless told to. Minds his own business. I let him out at night and no trouble."

"Now hold on, Bob. You say you let him out? You?"

"Sure. I bought him. He was the only goddamn one that done me a kindness."

I just looked at him. Seeing my expression, he said, "Think I'm crazy, huh? I got him for twenty-five bucks. Like I said, that German couple was fat, and their car was one of them squeezed-up beetle bugs. Put two stout people in it and that oversize dog, and you got a crowd. The Germans were glad to get him off their hands."

"I can see that."

"Days, I mostly keep him in the lean-to. Want to see him?"

"Do I have to lie down?"

"Not unless you're sleepy."

Studebaker went out the back and returned, followed by a horse. I sat still on my bar stool.

"Here's a friend, Gunnar," Studebaker said. "Go see nice friend. Jase, hold out your hand and let him sniff it."

I held it out, wondering what I would draw back. The dog sniffed it, gave it a lick and began wagging his stump of tail. He rested his head on my thigh. He could have put it on my shoulder without reaching.

I said, "Some dog, all right, Bob," and paid my bill and started for home. It wasn't the dog I kept thinking about. It wasn't police work or factions in town. Maybe Ike Doolittle would get me acquainted with her.

◆◆◆ 3 ◆◆◆

SHORT RIBS TWICE IN A ROW would revolt any appetite, unless my mother was one of the cooks. The grease in hers wouldn't have oiled a doll buggy. And she cooked them in beer. I wasn't interested in the rest of her methods, just in the results. Anyhow, she couldn't have explained in detail. She didn't measure by teaspoons or cups or fractions of them. A pinch of this, a tad of that, a splash of this, a shake of that. A born cook.

So I ate short ribs again. Over the meal I told Mother about Bob Studebaker and the oversize dog. She laughed but, being Mother, had to reflect, "Why, the poor man might have had a heart attack."

I helped with the dishes, and we went into the living room. I couldn't take my father's chair. I could see him there, reading, smiling once in a while and occasionally reading aloud a sentence or paragraph that struck him. Mother watched me and said, "He would want you to," but still I didn't sit in his chair. I thought I saw the beginning of tears in her eyes.

Break it up, I said to myself, and so I told her, "I'm on the night shift, Mother. You'll be all right alone?"

"Of course. Better than you'll be. Jase, do be careful."

I grinned to reassure her. "No danger. My instructions are to make friends."

"You're never in danger, according to you. Make friends with whom?"

"The newcomers. The strangers. The strip-mining crew."

"Everybody says they're riffraff. Make friends with them?" She sniffed. "They don't belong here."

"You can hear anything. They're human. Give them a chance."

I kissed her on the cheek, went into the hall and put on my down coat and earflapped cap. "You keep warm now," she said as I left her.

It was too early to visit the Chicken Shack, so, feeling shrunken with chill even in my down coat, I trailed down to the sheriff's office. It was empty except for Mrs. Lynn Carson, who sat at the switchboard, ready for phone calls or radio messages. She had a hearty manner and a little frame. It was as if the years, having taken some of her flesh, made up for it by strengthening her tongue.

"Deputy Beard reporting for duty," I said with a salute. "Make a note of the time."

"Deputy Tomfool," she answered, smiling. "What are you up to, down to, or into?"

"Classified instructions. I'm sworn not to blab."

"Make it exciting and report developments." She sighed. "I swear, a night like tonight, and a body could sit here and die, and the county no worse for it. One telephone call about a kitten up a pole. I said one of the town marshals would take care of that. Right?"

"Right." It was about all the town marshals, both of them, were up to.

"Tad Frazier's out in a cruiser. He reports nothing to report and wants to know can't he do something. That's all."

"Sheriff's not in?"

"He just left, late for dinner again. That poor man works too hard, and he's a man shy even with you here. You know Halvor Amussen's up at Petroleum, subbing for that deputy who broke his leg?"

I knew.

"What with conferences with the county commissioners, sheriff's sales, court hearings, managing this office and God knows what, Mr. Charleston has no time to himself. I bet he hasn't been to his country place in a month. Nights, he's on call at the Jackson Hotel. His wife might as well be a widow."

"She's with him."

"Of course, but what good does that do? Hardly a free moment with her alone, no time — never mind. I was just thinking."

"Not about law enforcement exactly," I said to fluster her.

She looked away from me and fiddled with a telephone cord. I imagined there was a blush under that aging skin. She said, "You just shut up, Jase," and went on, "I'm glad you're here to take part of the load."

"As much as I can."

I went to my desk in the sheriff's office and killed time. When the clock said nine-fifteen I went out to make friends.

Our town, like others on the high plains, just up and died early in bad winter weather. A few street lights burned, and here and there a dim gleam came from residences. Other windows were black, the people having gone to bed to keep

24

warm if nothing more. Up the street I could see the modest blue sign of the Bar Star. I supposed a couple of car engines were murmuring in front of it while the live ones went in for liver treatments.

In that still and bitter cold my footsteps rang on the walk, each step a ringing count of progress. Step and step and ring and ring in the echoing night. In town and all around, the earth was frozen six feet deep. The whole valley was a bell, and even boot heels swung the clapper.

A creek — Hill Creek officially — divides the town. The west side is the more respectable, or thinks it is. I walked east to the bridge. By contrast with the dimmed-out west, the sign above the Chicken Shack flamed on and off. The ice in the creek reflected changing shades of blue and red and yellow. Ahead the sign blazed over a place too small for it. BEER LIQUOR LIQUOR BEER ENTERTAINMENT.

Even through my earflapped cap noise stunned my ears as I opened the door. It was juke-box music or what went for music. I had outgrown rock 'n' roll, if ever I liked it. To me the singers sounded as if they had been raised by coyotes to the thump of Indian drums. The juke box hit its last licks just as I closed the door.

I took off my cap and then my coat, to reveal my badge, and hung them on a hook.

I advanced a few feet and stood while heads turned and sized me up. A half-dozen men, including Ike Doolittle, sat at the rough bar. Two women, looking sad and willing, were seated at a table, waiting, I supposed, for drinks to promote ideas. The men all wore head coverings, beaked caps mostly. The one nearest me was bristly and burly and had a chin that seemed to invite a fist. Just beyond him sat Ike and, two stools away, a muscled customer that I took to be Italian.

25

The burly man barely opened his mouth. "Do you see what I see?"

"Maybe I do," the man beyond Doolittle said. "An officer. That's what they call them here in the bush."

"Pig is the name." The burly customer looked me over, maybe to see whether I was armed. I wasn't. Charleston didn't approve of gun-toting except in emergencies. The man went on, "Something we can do for you?"

"I was looking for a quiet beer," I answered.

"Wrong place."

"What about whiskey then," I was straining myself to make friends.

The man turned farther on his stool. "What I mean to say is you're not welcome here. Better get out."

"You're the owner?"

"I'm the enforcer. Bouncer to you." His head turned briefly to the bartender. "Ain't that so, Pudge?"

The bartender's gaze was a mere slit, which was all that the fat of his face allowed. "Sure, Tim. Sure, when you're sober. Keep cool, man."

"Cool as a goddamn ice cube. That's me. But pigs melt me down."

The bar was silent. The women waited.

"No trouble now," the bartender said. His words sounded weak. "No trouble, please."

"It's no trouble at all." The hard blue eyes looked into mine. "I said go. I said get out."

"When I'm ready," I told him.

"Now!" He swung off his stool and ran at me. He swung with his left. I dodged, caught his wrist and used his own momentum to fling him behind me. His head hit the door with a satisfying thump.

From the side of my eye I saw the Italian type making for me, a beer bottle aloft in his hand. I saw him, and I saw Doolittle stick out his foot. The man tripped and fell on his face.

I had heard of a monkey on a man's back, meaning something else, but now I witnessed it. Doolittle jumped to the man's shoulders and sat astride, his own beer bottle lifted. When the man tried to buck him off, Doolittle said, "Down Mussolini," and hit him on the head. Mussolini went down.

The saloon was silent. The other customers watched, with what feelings I couldn't tell. The two women sat forward, eager, as if they hadn't known such excitement since they entered the trade.

The man I had thrown climbed to his feet. His hand went to his head. Tottering a little, he turned around and said to me, "A goddamn pro, huh?"

"I've taken a few lessons."

"Next time I'll know." He took his seat at the bar.

"Gimme a glass of ice water," Doolittle said to the bartender. He took the glass and poured the water over the head of the man he had conked. The man twitched and snorted and finally got up. He made his way to a stool, the fight gone out of him. "Jesus Christ," he complained to Doolittle, "you didn't have to hit me so hard." He took off his cap and rubbed his skull.

"I couldn't figure how much bone was there."

"I'll tie you in a knot one of these days."

"Maybe so," Doolittle said, unperturbed. "The answer lies in the future, or, to make it plain to you, time will tell."

It struck me that there was some inner confidence in the little man, some inner resolution, some sure faith in himself that, reflecting outward, earned him, if not command, then a wary respect. Perhaps he had tangled with one of these hard-hats before.

"What's your name?" I asked the burly man, my notebook and pencil in hand.

"Find out for yourself."

"It's Tim Reagan," Doolittle told me cheerfully.

"And yours?" I asked the man who was still feeling the bump the beer bottle had made.

"Regular League of Nations here," Doolittle said. "Name of this friend is Tony Coletti."

"Why don't you keep your mouth shut?" the bartender asked Doolittle.

"Aw, you with the fat face, pipe down."

I had scribbled down the names of the two men, as given by Doolittle. Watching, he asked brightly, "Going to take them in?"

I said, "Naw, naw. Just a friendly fracas. Bartender, set 'em up."

The men accepted their drinks, all but Reagan and Coletti. Passing me on the way out, Reagan said, "Next time. Always a next time."

"Sorry I had to bust you."

"In a pig's ass. Yours."

I gulped a beer, and Doolittle tossed off a drink. I said to him, "Better come with me."

"Why so?"

"Your friends here might be mad at you."

"Not right," he answered. "Just stand up for yourself, and they let you alone. But I'll come along, anyhow."

We went to the sheriff's office, and I talked to him at length, trying to figure him out, wondering. I didn't get very far.

"Why did you get involved?" I asked at last. "Why did you take sides with me?"

"Oh, hell," he answered. "They figured to gang you, and me,

I usually take the side of the law, or the underdog, anyhow."
He added, after consideration, "Big guys, big arrogant bas-
tards, they bug me. I'm so small, see?"

He left after a while, and I spent the rest of the night half-
drowsing at my desk. It was just as well, I thought, that nothing was happening, and I was one whale of a success making
friends.

Mother woke me up, saying Mr. Leonard Willsie wanted to talk to me. Mr. Willsie, a long-time associate of my father in the abstract business, had taken over the office on my father's death. I threw on a robe, more against the chill than for modesty, and went to the phone.

It was still dark, maybe 7:30 a.m. I said, "Good morning, Mr. Willsie," not seeing anything particularly good about it.

"Welcome home, Jason," he told me. "I understand you are working in the sheriff's office again?"

"Yes, sir."

"That's why I called you. I don't know Mr. Charleston too well. Someone has shattered my window."

"At the office? The big plate-glass window?"

"Yes. With bricks. He left a note. Or they did."

"I'll be right along."

Pausing an instant before I went into the bedroom to dress, I answered the question on Mother's face. "Hooligans," I said. "They broke Mr. Willsie's window. All right. Our window, formerly ours. No. Breakfast later, please."

The office occupied all of a small building that stood at the head of Main Street, a little remote from other enterprises. Mr. Willsie was waiting for me in front of the wrecked window. There was a big hole in it, jagged with shards of glass. Mr. Willsie was a gray, good man with eyes strained by peering at figures and documents. Before ever I knew him he had suffered from polio and now got around with difficulty, helped by a leg brace and a cane.

He shook hands, saying, "You can see the damage, Jason. Come inside, not that it's much warmer there."

We entered, crunching glass, and stood beside a desk and rows of files. I asked, "Was anything stolen, Mr. Willsie?"

He gestured with his free hand. "Not a thing. Nothing disturbed. The door was still locked, and I doubt that anyone would have tried to get in through that broken hole."

"You spoke of a note?"

He took a piece of crumpled paper from the top of the desk and handed it to me. "It was wrapped around a brick that apparently was thrown in after the glass was broken."

On the coarse paper, written in block capitals, appeared the words LAY OFF OR TAKE THE CONSEQUENCES.

I asked the natural question. "Have you reason to suspect anybody?"

He nodded his head slowly. "I must suppose it was one of the strip miners."

"Why?"

"I oppose strip mining, Jason. I do not want to see our land despoiled. I stated my reasons for opposition in a letter to the paper last week. Maybe you saw it?"

"No, sir."

"It was a reasoned and temperate statement and invited

comment." His hand went toward the broken window. "But not this!"

The hand continued in a gesture of weary distress. "Decisions should be reached through calm reason, not senseless violence. What is happening to us, Jase? What will happen?"

I was short of any answers and so said, "I'll report to Mr. Charleston, and we'll do our best. Meantime, can we help you? Get someone to board up the window? Order new glass?"

He tried to smile. "Thank you, Jason. I'm still capable of using the telephone."

It was a sort of rebuke for tactless questions. I went on. "Of course, Mr. Willsie. I suppose you'll take an enforced holiday today. It's mighty cold in this room."

"One of the inner offices will be snug enough."

I left him leaning on his cane, his head bowed, and walked to the office. Charleston had just arrived. I told him what had happened and gave him the note, saying, "Naturally, Mr. Willsie thinks it was one of the strip miners."

"It could be the reverse. Someone who wanted to inflame sentiment against them."

"I suppose so."

"We may never find out who did it, Jase. Witnesses? Late at night in bitter weather? Noise heard from a building separated from others?" His head moved as if to shake a thought from it. It was plain the thought wouldn't shake out, for he continued, "I'm afraid this is a portent. Things to come, Jase. Things to come."

"Anyhow," I said, "now that I'm up I might as well stay for a while."

"If you choose to."

"I have to tell you about last night, but, first, maybe I have an idea."

"It wouldn't be the first time. Spill it, Jase."

"About a deputy, I mean."

"Well?"

"You'll just laugh."

"Good. I like to laugh. Who is it?" He raised an eyebrow. "Out with it, boy."

"It's Ike Doolittle."

"That's a laugh all right," he answered, not laughing. "The whole county will bust its seams."

"Maybe."

"You can't be serious. That Gulley Jimson!"

"Yes, sir. Call him what you want to."

Charleston spread his hands. "A strong wind, and where is he? Flying to Dakota, that's where. Let a tough customer face him, and where would he be? Disabled or dead or on the run."

"I've seen him in action, Mr. Charleston."

"So?"

I told him then, with no adornments but no slighting of facts, about the fracas at the Chicken Shack and, when he didn't respond at once, ended lamely. "I guess I'm not such a good hand at making friends."

At last he spoke. "I imagine he has a record."

"Not according to him. I sounded him out."

"I hope you didn't suggest a job here." At the shake of my head, he added, "By the evidence we have, a boozer to boot."

"I think we're wrong there. He says liquor's no problem."

"They all do."

"All right," I said. "It was just an idea."

Charleston put a match to one of his thin cigars and sat thinking. Then he said through the smoke, "Tad Frazier was one of your ideas, too. Glad I acted on it."

"Thanks."

"I've been known to be wrong." That good smile of his came to his face. "You've got me half persuaded. To talk to him, anyhow. Know where to find this giant killer?"

"I can look."

"Make it late this afternoon, Jase. Go get some breakfast if you haven't had any. Take a nap. Then bring him along, will you?"

I went home and ate and, thinking I couldn't get to sleep, snoozed along until dusk. I took time to shave, bathe, eat a bite and talk a while with Mother .

I didn't have to look long for Ike Doolittle. He was eating at the Commercial Cafe and had a couple of bites of a hamburger left. There was ketchup on his whiskers. I resisted a prejudice against people who drenched their food with that stuff.

"The sheriff would like to talk to you," I told him right off.

He used a paper napkin, which came away looking like a used hospital dressing. "Oh, Lord, what have I done?"

I smiled to reassure him, though he seemed not to need reassurance. "Nothing serious, as far as I know."

"What have I left undone?"

"Paying the bill here. Give me your tab."

While I paid it, he wrestled his sheepskin coat on. The only words said as we walked to the office were mine. "Nothing to be alarmed about. It's not a charge."

Charleston rose when we entered his office. "How are you, Mr. Doolittle?" he asked, his eyes busy. "Have off your coat and take a seat."

With Doolittle seated, he went on. "I wanted to thank you personally for helping Jase last night."

"He could have managed alone, but I didn't want to miss the fun. A good time was had by all."

34

"With two exceptions."

"As the politician says, you can't please everybody."

I wondered whether the remark was a sly dig, the sheriff's office being elective. I couldn't tell through the whiskers. Doolittle took out a red bandana and wiped the melting frost from them. "Anyhow, your thanks accepted with thanks, but do I have to beware of the Greeks bearing gifts?"

Charleston said, "Nothing like that." He looked at Doolittle so long, head to foot, that even Doolittle had to squirm slightly. "I didn't have time to dress for inspection or tidy my whiskers," Doolittle told him.

"Sorry. They're cold-weather protection?"

"Not a disguise, that's for sure, if that's what you're thinking. Come spring, off they go."

"Or sooner, part of them at least, if advisable?"

"Like a judge, I would have to take the case under consideration. But why ask me, if I may be so bold as to ask?"

The switchboard broke in, and Charleston didn't get to reply then. Mrs. Carson's voice said, clear enough for me to hear, "A man's here to report a shooting."

"Send him in."

The visitor entered. I thought of Christmas trees, those frosted over with phony white. Bristles of beard stood out on his face like sprayed needles.

"A man's hurt. Shot. Needs help."

The man was young and big, made bigger by his heavy clothing.

"Shot where?"

"In the foot. Clear through."

Charleston's half-sigh meant exasperation. "I mean where is he?"

"In his tent. All alone."

35

"Sit down, boy. Warm up. One thing at a time now. Who are you?"

The man sat on the edge of a chair and ran his mittened hand over his face. "I'm a backpacker."

"Name?"

"Peterson. Pete."

"Backpacking in this weather?"

"It wasn't so bad the other side of the divide. But look, I came to find help!"

"Where's the tent the man's in?"

"The south fork of Rose River, quite a ways up, near the end of the road."

"How did he get shot?"

"I forgot. A robber shot him and took off."

"That's what he told you?"

"Yes." Peterson seemed a little easier now. "It was earlier this morning he got shot."

"When did you find him?"

"It must have been about noon. I dropped my pack off and hiked in. Not a damn car on the road."

"Will we need an ambulance?"

"I don't think so. He was sitting up with his bloody foot stretched out when I left. I filled his water pail out of the creek and brought in some wood and put it close to the camp stove where he could reach it, and then I took off."

"No horses around?"

"None that I saw."

"There's a dude ranch not far away."

"I didn't notice. I just kept hoofing."

Charleston turned to me. "Jase, you know that road. Pick up Old Doc Yak. I'll alert him. If it seems best, stop at the dude ranch and tell Guy Jamison to be on the lookout. He can

36

call his neighbors." By "neighbors" he meant people who lived from five to ten miles away. "Only if it seems best. Use your own judgment."

"I'll go, too," Peterson put in.

"No. Stay in town. You've had enough. Jase will pick up your pack."

I left the three of them there in the office. Doolittle looked as if he wanted to come along, but one deep thinker, meaning Old Doc Yak, would be enough company for me.

I went out and scratched the ice from the windshield of the police car, unhooked the electric cord from the engine heater, and started the engine. I turned the blower on defrost but still had to keep wiping a peephole through the mist my breath made on the glass. I might as well be looking through binoculars, I thought as I drove.

Doc Yak was waiting for me when I pulled up in front of his place. He came out when he saw the lights, his satchel in his hand.

"Suffering Jesus and goddamn that Charleston," he said as he got into the car. "Why in hell did I ever take up medicine?"

He didn't wear a down coat. His was of old, heavy wool that reached to his knees. He had a scarf wound around his neck and black earmuffs under his hat.

"Why did I take this job?" I answered him. I had the car under way.

"Idiots, both of us. Idiots in occupation as well as location in a country where polar bears freeze their balls off. Idiots." He made a swipe at the windshield though most of the mist had cleared off.

"Shot in the foot in a tent, huh?" he said, not indicating a change in subject. He never did. He just let his mind hop around.

"By a robber. That's what the man said."

"What man?"

"A backpacker who stumbled onto the scene."

After a silence Doc said, "Jase, you give me new faith in myself."

"How's that?"

"A tenter and a backpacker! In this weather! We aren't the only fools, my boy. We're not even the biggest fools. By comparison we're brains, and God loves us."

He settled back as if satisfied with his intellectual rating.

Abruptly he sat forward and asked, "In the foot, huh?"

"That's our information."

He made a noise in his throat and slumped back again.

Not so long ago the road we followed had been a bone-rattler, boulders alternating with holes, and man and machine suffered from it, from traveling what realists had called "that rocky-ass road." But since then the county had paved most of it, and we made good time. The night was clear and dead. Along the sides of the pavement vegetation stood stiff, as if it had seen its last season. Only the stars, winking at the frozen world, gave some appearance of life.

We turned left where the road forked, and our wheels crunched on gravel. We crossed the main-river bridge and turned right, headed for the canyon of the South Fork. An animal — a frost-bitten deer, I made out — jumped from the borrow pit and crossed in front of us. Two others followed. I had to brake sharp for them. Doc murmured, "Venison."

Guy Jamison's dude ranch was dark. I drove on without stopping. Six miles more, and I saw the tent. A dim light shone through the canvas.

We got out there, Doc with his satchel and I with a flashlight that I turned on, directing its beam here and there as we walked. The tent was shored up with clods, muddied sticks, and dirt. At the sides of the flapped entrance there were grouse feathers and rabbit skins.

"Anybody home?" I called out.

Words that I couldn't distinguish answered the call. I entered the tent, Doc right behind me. There was a lingering warmth in the place, coming from a sheet-iron camp stove. A man on a low cot reared up and asked, "Who are you?"

I replied, "Rescue squad," and took a quick look around while Doc went to the patient. Besides the stove, the tent was fitted with a rough table, a counter made of planks laid across makeshift trestles, a couple of wood blocks for seats, a bucket of water on another block, a lighted lantern that sat on the table, and the cot on which the man now half-lay. Angled against a corner was a small-caliber rifle. Near it were a couple of apple boxes used for shelves. A couple of paper bags rested on them.

"I'm a doctor," Doc said. "How's the foot?"

"Hurts like hell." The man was dressed, except for his feet. He didn't appear either big or small. He could have done with a razor, could have done with it, say, a month ago.

"Gunshot wounds usually do. Let me look at the foot. Jase, see about some hot water."

A pot already was on the stove, pretty well filled. I put a couple of sticks in the firebox.

Doc was unwinding the bloody rag from around the man's foot. He said, "Shine your flashlight over here, Jase."

When I had focused it, Doc tried feeling the foot, to find broken bones if any, I supposed.

The man let out "Ouch."

More to distract him than extract information, I asked, "What's your name?"

"Tuttle. Kingston Tuttle."

"Be damned if I ever expected to work on King Tut," Doc said.

Tuttle let out a sudden yelp of pain. He followed it with "Leave out your old wit and the shit."

"Such language I never heard from a king."

I asked, "Where you from?"

"Anywhere you say."

"Hot water ready, Jase?"

"Right here." I felt the heat of the pot through my mitt.

Doc opened his satchel and got out what he needed. "Lucky," he told the man. "Clean wound. No bones broken, I think. Maybe bruised." With soap from his bag and water from the pot, he was cleaning the bloody foot, having first rubbed alcohol on his hands. The water was too hot for immediate application. He would take a piece of gauze, hold on to a corner, dip the gauze in the water and then wave it around before using it.

I looked up from the foot. "A man shot you, you said?"

"That's what I said."

"Can you describe him? What did he look like?"

"You don't take notes with a hole in your foot. Don't bug me. Medium, just all-around medium, that's what he was."

"You reported he robbed you. What did he take?"

"I don't know. Not much to take."

"Your rifle?" I asked.

"I guess he didn't see it."

Doc was preparing a hypodermic.

"What were, what are, you doing here?"

"Look around, for God's sake. Camping. Living with nature. Living off nature."

Doc said, "King Tut becomes Henry David Thoreau. Remarkable transformation. Bare your arm, Henry."

"What's that for?" Tuttle asked, looking at the needle.

"Against tetanus, known to the laity as lockjaw."

As he put away the needle, Doc said, "Dipper of water, Jase." At about the same time, he took a tablet from a vial. "Swallow this."

"Why?"

"So you can go camping again, Henry. You'll need two legs."

After Tuttle had washed down the pill, Doc said, "All right. Now friends, we take sad leave of Walden Pond."

We bundled Tuttle up. Doc put his cold-weather gear back on. I looked around for Peterson's backpack and found it behind the stove wood. On second thought I stepped to where the rifle stood and took it in my hand.

"Hey," Tuttle said, "that's mine."

"Want it stolen? That robber might come again."

We managed to put Tuttle into the car, along with the pack and the rifle, and set out for town. Guy Jamison's dude ranch was still dark. I didn't stop there.

"To my office," Doc told me. Those were almost the only words spoken on our way back to town.

We laid Tuttle out in one of the two rooms Doc kept for emergency patients. "I'll be here a while," he informed me, "if Charleston wants to call."

Charleston was waiting for me, and I made my report.

"Did you wake up the Jamisons? Ask them to watch out?"

"No, sir. It didn't seem worth it."

"Your decision. Good enough for me."

He called Doc and talked for a minute, then said, "Come on, Jase."

Doc didn't greet us or ask any questions. He just opened the door and said, "He'll be hobbling around before you know it. Jase knows where he is."

Tuttle was wide awake. Doc had put quite a bandage on his foot. On the night stand were a glass, a pitcher of water and a bottle of pills.

He frowned at us. "Can't you let a man rest?"

Charleston took the one chair in the room, and I stood. "Soon enough." Charleston spoke shortly. "My deputy here has asked you some questions. I have some more." He leaned toward the bed and went on, his words building up like a lawyer's summation. "You can't describe the robber, you don't know what he took, and you were shot in the foot."

Tuttle moved back in the bed, taking care with his foot. "That's right."

"I find it funny."

"You wouldn't with a bullet hole in you."

"Let's talk about that hole. What position were you in when he fired?"

"You expect me to remember?"

"You were standing up?"

"Not after he shot me."

"Now the doctor tells me that the bullet went almost straight down, almost vertical, top of your foot to the bottom. Explain that."

"I won't. I can't."

"I can. You were holding the rifle in your own hands, holding it butt up and muzzle down, and you were careless. You shot yourself. If I could think of a charge, I'd be tempted to run you in."

Charleston had spoken with a harshness unusual for him,

but it served its purpose. Tuttle broke. He brought his hands to his face, groaned and said, "Oh, Jesus! It's all spoiled."

We waited for him to go on.

"I said I could live off nature. I promised to prove it. Thoreau did."

Charleston's gaze came to me, and he said under his breath, "With many a square meal at the Emersons."

"Call me a nature freak, but I believe in the primitive life. That's how I want to live, away from men and their problems and their artificial creations. Back to the old days, the good days, the days of our ancestors."

Sentimentality was hard for Charleston to take. Me, too. Hysteria was worse. But we listened.

A whimper escaped Tuttle. "I told people I could do it. I bet I could do it. I made a big thing of it. Don't you see? Don't you see? What will they think of me? What will they say of me now? Just crazy. Just another oddball. Had this idiotic notion, and look where it got him. Laugh. Laugh."

Charleston said, "Time to go, Jase."

❖❖❖ 5 ❖❖❖

I WAS MAKING IT A POINT, though not on instructions, to be in the office in time to talk to Charleston. Now, at the switchboard, Blanche Burton halted me. "You'd never believe it, Jase," she said. "Never in this world. He's a dear man."

"No doubt about it," I answered.

"Guess who?"

"Don't I fit the picture?"

"Go along with you. It's the new deputy."

"News to me," I told her. It wasn't really, now that she had spoken. "Who might this darling man be?"

"That's not for me to tell. It's for you to find out. I almost fell over."

I had a notion to say, "Backwards, of course," but didn't. A man thinks a lot of things he doesn't express. "When will I meet this fine specimen?"

She waved. "Just go through the door."

I almost fell over myself when I saw Ike Doolittle. He wore over new boots a new pair of pants, creased, and a good wool shirt. Gone were his whiskers except for a trim mustache. He looked younger and somehow bigger. Whereas I had thought, when he took off that old sheepskin coat, it was like peeling a peach to get at the pit, now in his new clothes and a short-waisted jacket the pit was filling its covering. I had time, too, to notice the breadth of his shoulders. He was still short, of course, maybe five feet four, but I put his weight at 130 pounds or close to it.

He saluted me. "Sergeant Doolittle of the Northwest Mounted Police." He stood near the desk at which Charleston was seated.

Charleston shied a smile at me. "All right, Ike," he said. "Check on Tuttle and take the pack to the backpacker, then check back in."

"Yes, sir." Doolittle put on a new down coat and a new pair of furred gloves. I imagined Charleston had advanced money for the whole outfit. It would be like him. Doolittle went out, carrying the pack.

"So?" I said to Charleston as I seated myself.

"So it is. I think your hunch will work out. We'll see. He hardly needed instructions about operations. I'll put him in a cruiser."

"No cruiser for me?"

"When you require one, of course, but for the most part I want you to be in easy reach. For important things."

I took his words for a compliment. "It turned out last night wasn't so important."

He yawned, needing sleep, I supposed. "It was important for Tuttle, the fool, and important for us in a way, part of our duty. We just couldn't let him lie there in his tent."

"I know that."

"Sure you do. And you know that half and more of our job is just chasing rabbits."

A call came for him then. He said "Yes" into the phone and listened. "All right. He insists, huh? Go on. Take him back out."

He hung up and explained to me, with a motion toward the phone. "Ike. We're delivering rabbits now. Peterson wants to go back to that tent."

"Back?"

"Yeah. Yeah. Seems he swore he would backpack to Minneapolis, and he can't count the trip from the tent into town because he didn't have his pack with him. Matter of conscience." He shook his head. His smile was twisted.

"Two of a kind, he and Tuttle," I said.

"Not quite, Jase. Tuttle's first thought was to save face. God spare us from such. Makes wars, face-saving does." He rose and put on his wraps. "Take over, boy."

It developed there wasn't much to take over. I talked to Tad Frazier over the radio. He was hot, he thought, on the trail of a stolen car. I took the license number and relayed it to Doolittle. After midnight the owner of a beer-and-snack joint just south of town reported someone somehow had made off with a hundred-dollar bill. I asked him if he had left the cash drawer open. He couldn't remember. I asked when. He couldn't remember when either. He'd just found out. I asked about suspects. He didn't want to accuse anybody. I told him a deputy would be right out. I thought of going myself but decided in favor of Doolittle. The man probably had just misplaced the money. No suspects? On a freezing night when customers would have been mighty few? Let Doolittle chase the rabbit.

I drowsed at my desk, to be wakened by Halvor Amussen, calling from Petroleum. Nothing doing there except that the cold was breaking records. He just wanted to talk, making sure someone was alive.

I went out to the switchboard and talked to Mrs. Carson for a while, or, rather, she talked to me. Then I napped some more and went home.

❖❖❖ 6 ❖❖❖

For the next two days, or, rather, nights, I didn't earn my keep. I came to work. I stayed. I napped. I stood ready to answer calls, but few came in and these were unimportant. Neither did anyone else do anything but put in time, save for the sheriff. Three women, one of whom I hadn't met, manned — or womaned — the switchboard and radio, which largely were silent. Tad Frazier took over the day shift, Ike Doolittle the night, and I filled in as the schedule demanded. Mostly we hung around the office, saving gasoline, glad to be out of the cold, and talked and drank the coffee the women kept brewing. Ike reported that the hundred-dollar bill had been found. The owner's wife had taken it for safekeeping, not wanting their cash reserve to mingle with common currency. We were all a drag on the economy.

Again except for the sheriff. What with correspondence, record keeping, attendance at meetings and other dull chores, he was occupied.

Even so, I had a sense of impending developments, and so,

I thought, did Charleston. Off and on I had another mutilated animal to think about, this time across the line in Canada. And the victim wasn't a cow or steer. It was a pony. Who would want to kill a pony? For what reason? The devil with those speculations. No mutilations made sense.

But it wasn't that report that promoted our mood. It may have been the unnatural quiet in the town, a quiet that the cold alone couldn't account for. To walk the streets was to see almost nobody, least of all strip miners. I walked them and thought about a movie in which a man found buildings and standing homes but not one living being, human or animal.

It wasn't until late Monday afternoon that Charleston told me, "Jase, there's that environmental meeting tonight. I think you should be there."

I knew about the meeting. It was to be held in the high-school auditorium with some official presiding.

I said, "It'll give me something to do, at least."

He opened a desk drawer and brought out a file. "It's a state hearing, aimed at sounding out public sentiment about strip mining, but I'm sure some federal men will be there, representing the Bureau of Land Management. Both state and federal acreage is involved, as well as some private land already leased. But here." He thrust the file at me. "No need to tell you."

Before he said good-bye, leaving me with the file, he said, "Things might get hot."

From the file I learned that the boosters for mining would have as their lead spokesman one Arthur Oldham, a public-relations officer for Energy Associates. One circular referred to him as Oily Arthur, saying Energy Associates was the child of Texas oil interests. Opposing him would be Judge John Church.

The local chamber of commerce sided with the coal people. Naturally, I thought. Already I had come to the conviction that businessmen had the foresight of moles.

After the opening statements, the file informed me, the hearing would be opened to general discussion.

Shortly before eight o'clock I bundled up and walked to the high school. Maybe two dozen cars were already parked close by, and others were nosing in. So a sizable crowd would attend, maybe not altogether because of the issue. Winter-bound people always welcomed a good excuse to get out. What if that frigid air nipped at the lungs and frosted the nostrils? What if cars wouldn't start later? Here was something going on. Here was a diversion, here something to do, even if not so important as a basketball game.

A rough count showed fifty people were already in the auditorium, and others were arriving as I finished the tally. Tim Reagan and Tony Coletti, my friends the strip miners, were on hand. So was Chuck Cleaver, the rancher, his usually friendly face creased with concern.

A desk had been placed on the floor below the stage, where the curtain was closed. No theater then. Just informality. A man sat at the desk, waiting. Close to him was another man I took to be the official reporter. He didn't have anything on me. I had my note pad and a couple of pencils and enough knowledge of shorthand to keep pace. In the front row four other strangers sat. They would be officials, state and federal.

As the last stragglers settled themselves, the man at the desk rapped with a gavel and announced, "Attention, please. This is a state meeting, called in accordance with the law. Its purpose is to hear and later assess the pros and cons of the application of Energy Associates to strip mine certain sections of the county." He held up a map. "Those of you who want to determine the areas in question may do so by coming to the desk later." He put the map down. "My name is William Gregg. The state has appointed me as the hearing officer."

He paused and looked the crowd over. "First we shall have the opening statements and then throw the meeting open to general discussion. The proponents will be heard now. May I introduce Mr. Arthur Oldham, their spokesman?"

From the front row Oldham got up and faced the crowd. He let us study him for a moment, let us take in his considerable heft, his friendliness, his easy assurance. He had the look about him of good drinks, thick steaks and dollar cigars. "May it please you," he said, as if sure it would, his hands making an open gesture of welcome, "I am aware that the issue in point has aroused controversy. I hope to calm it. I hope by candid discussion and the presentation of facts to allay fears."

He lifted his eyes to the ceiling and found higher communion beyond it. "I think with awe of this great country of ours. Back through the years of history I see a little cluster of colonies on the eastern shore. I see them growing. I see the brave push of Americans into the wilderness, and I see that wilderness conquered and made fruitful and the blessings of civilization introduced from sea to shining sea."

He took off the horn-rimmed glasses he wore and extended them toward us. If we looked through them, maybe we could see what he saw. A voice back of me called out, "Get to the subject!"

Oldham put the glasses back on his nose. "I am on the subject, my friend. Only by taking the long view can we place the issue in perspective. I ask you what is the secret of our once and continuing greatness? What has made us the greatest nation on God's green earth? The answer lies plain before us. It is growth. It is onward development. It is the plain fact of bigger and better. To come down to cases, then, it is the wise use of our natural resources. It is energy, the energy of individuals and the energy they can create from what God has given. We in this area have been given coal, great beds of it lying just under the sod."

Oldham allowed time for his words to sink in. With an arm extended he went on. "It is ours, we may say. It belongs to us and no others. Let us hang on to it. But in all conscience may we say that? What if the state of Minnesota had kept closed for its own use alone the iron ore of the great Mesabi Range? What would our factories have done for steel? What would you farmers and ranchers have employed in place of machinery? Wooden plows? Plodding horses? What if each state so blessed had held to itself the great pine forests, growing there not for the sake of a select few but for all Americans that they might have shelter? What if our own state had withheld from our country the deposits of gold, silver and, yes, copper that the Almighty had stored in our boundaries?"

Oldham paused to think about those dread possibilities. While he thought, someone yelled, "You're not from Montana. Bullshit!"

The dirty word was not a fitting expression in a public meeting, not in our town, not in the presence of women, of whom quite a few were on hand. It put a hush on the crowd. I suspected Chuck Cleaver had uttered it.

The chairman rapped with his gavel.

Oldham wasn't flustered at all. "Let us forgive that unseemly outburst," he said, lowering his head and his voice as if he forgave. "It is true that I am not a Montanan, but I am an American and proud of it, and Montana is part of America, and you may be proud that it is."

He got down to what he called particulars then. He talked

about the jobs that mining would create, of local men steadily and productively employed. He spoke of flourishing businesses. He saw our town growing happily, in time becoming a small city, a place where everyone would find satisfaction.

He asked that a screen be brought from the side of the hall and, with help from a colleague who served as projectionist, showed pictures taken where strip mining was being done. The pictures were of loaded coal cars streaming away from the mines, of spoil banks reclaimed and the rich graze that grew on them.

The screen was wheeled away, and Oldham launched into his finish. "Let us return, then, to what I said earlier. It is to the credit of each state, in these, the United States, that it has been willing and eager to share what it has. None has been so selfish, so parochial, as to claim its riches for itself alone. Our progress, our lives as we know them, have been built on a simple dogma, on a prime principle. Each for all is our creed. Yes, each for all." His hands went out, pleading. "In all conscience, then, can Montana deny to others the riches with which she is blessed? Can she say no to progress, no to growth, no to energy? Can she say no to coal? God help us, God save us from that wayward course?"

God helping him, he made his slow way back to his chair. The crowd gave him quite a hand, a deserved hand, I thought. Even a prejudiced witness like me had to admit he had made a good case, even though he had had to call on God, the flag and ripe prose to do it. Yet the applause seemed polite — no, restrained — as if sentiments ran too deep for foot stomping or shouted amens. No matter. He would be a hard number to follow. I looked at my watch. He had spoken for more than an hour.

The chairman asked if there were other official spokesmen

for the proponents. Harry Wallace, president of the Chamber of Commerce got up. He sold hardware. He stood where he was and, under the hypnosis of the cash register, said, "I represent the Chamber of Commerce, and I say for all members that we stand solid behind what just has been said."

"Other official spokesmen?" the chair asked. When no one answered, he nodded and announced, "We will hear from the opponents, then. I understand Judge Church has been nominated. Judge Church, the floor is yours."

I had a speaking acquaintance with Judge Church, that was all. He was a small man, frail in appearance, who was born, I sometimes thought, with a clean collar and a knotted necktie, plus a freshly pressed suit. Already well along in years, he had retired to Montana after what was said to be a distinguished legal career in the East. My father had admired him.

For a moment, facing us, he stood silent, his eyes going from one to another like those of a man making sure he would know us the next time we met. I put his age at the late seventies, a stage when the years would have shrunken his body as they had written themselves on his face. He was no physical match for Oldham, no match except for the eyes that bored at us from under a thatch of white hair.

"How long will we feed on a fallacy?" he asked, so softly that we strained to hear him. "How long will the old myth bemuse us?" Now he raised his voice. "How long can we live by a lie?"

He repeated, "How long?" one old hand open in a question. "That fallacy, that myth, that lie, my friends, is the doctrine that bigger means better, that growth is the answer to all human ills. Growth. Mere physical growth. On that basis it is not too ridiculous to say that you would be better people if you had grown bigger every year of your lives." The suggestion of

54

a smile touched his mouth. "The dinosaurs tried that," he said, leaving us to think what had happened to them. Some in the crowd chuckled.

"We are cursed with the notion that quantity leads on to quality, that size has a merit built in. New York City is superior to Chicago, then, Chicago superior to Detroit, and all of them, plus hundreds of others, superior to us. Far superior just because they are bigger. What nonsense!"

He took a breath and changed gears. "We have coal in this county. There is no doubt about that. We know it. The corporations know it even better, what with their explorations, their test holes and all. As eastern Montana has coal, so do we. You have just seen pictures of that eastern Montana coal being shipped out by train. Shipped out to where? To other sections, of course. That has been the history of Montana. We have given our great riches, our wealth of minerals, we have given them to outside interests for little in return. Gold and silver and copper have made millionaires of men who live elsewhere. Montanans have been the working stiffs, the day-by-day laborers, while men from afar have grown fat. Throughout the years we have existed, not as a state, but as a colony. We supply the raw materials and pay dearly for what has been manufactured from them. Except for our wealth of coal, we are just about out of riches now. Gold is gone, silver is gone, and copper is going, and what do we have to show for them? Dead camps, dead dreams, and one moldering city."

He took a couple of steps to one side and then back, his head lowered. Then he raised it and fixed us with that aimed gaze of his. "Mr. Oldham also has shown you pictures of what is said to be reclaimed land — pictures of soil banks dozed down and canyoned trenches filled in and all of it made level and planted to grasses. The grasses grow thick. They grow tall.

But at what cost in fertilizer and water? At a cost no rancher could ever afford. Never in all his life, no matter the market for livestock. Left to nature, those grasses will die, and never again will our native forage flourish on those ruined fields."

Judge Church went to the desk for a swallow of water and returned. His voice as he resumed showed no sign of fatigue. It was still clear and carrying, with no quaver of age in it. "Mr. Oldham has spoken of local prosperity, of business and sales and jobs and increased general welfare. The records of other mining camps reveal other consequences. They reveal shantytowns, growing disorder, increased crime and additional taxes. You should look at those records. Look at Gillette or Rock Springs, both in Wyoming. Look and pay heed."

He had had the floor for some time but still wasn't through. No one seemed fidgety. Except for a cough now and then, all were silent and attentive. "Granted an immediate growth in business and jobs if mining is permitted," he continued, "we must ask how long will this blush of prosperity last. An honest answer is thirty years, thirty years and no longer. Thirty years, and we are left despoiled. We are left a wasteland where nothing can grow, where no livestock can find graze. I exaggerate. Maybe a goat or two could live on the weeds."

He got a few murmurs from that last remark. Most of them seemed to be in approval.

He still hadn't finished. He resumed in a slower, musing tone. "I was present when my grandfather died. On his death-bed he said to me, 'I am about to join the great majority.' With those words he passed on."

Judge Church took time to look us all over again. His voice strengthened. "Today my grandfather couldn't say what he did then. He would have to say he was joining the minority party. Hard to believe as it is, there are more people alive on the planet now than all those who ever died on it. More alive now than all those who have gone before. More alive than ever perished through famines, wars, pestilences, disasters and natural causes. More than all our forefathers in the whole history of man. We are become an infestation on our small planet. We are devouring it. Continent by continent, country by country, state by state, piece by piece, we are eating it up. We are too many, too numerous for earth to support. And yet we hear hymns to growth. Growth, the way of death!"

A hoarse voice rose in back of me. "Just a minute now!"

I hitched around. The speaker was Jim Burke, a sometime auto mechanic and the father of ten or twelve kids. I doubted he knew the exact number.

Judge Church said, "Yes?" and waited.

"We came here to talk coal, and here you are talking about birth control and sterilization and abortion and all that damn stuff. It's unGodly."

Judge Church held up his hand. "My concern with growth may have led me a little afield, but I am not aware that I spoke of those matters."

"Just the same as did."

The chairman rapped with his gavel to no effect. The man remained standing. Judge Church fixed his eyes on him. "Since you bring the subject up, let me say that, for his own sake and the sake of the world around him, the person who cannot control his carnal appetite indeed needs the help of science."

After those words, to the rapping of the gavel, Burke sat down.

"One minute more, and I am through," Judge Church told us. "Mr. Oldham with his oratory never tackled the real issue here, and I have only touched on it. The issue is not whether we are selfish or parochial, as he has suggested. It is not that we want to keep the coal for ourselves, and to the devil with everyone else. We want, we opponents want, to save a way of life, the way of the rancher and grain grower. We are concerned with the soil, the good earth that nourishes plant, animal, and man and will nourish us forever if we love and care for it. Disturb it, as strip mining does, turn over its crust, dig in its bowels, and it dies, never to be raised from the dead. Destroy and perish, boom and bust — what an outlook!"

He turned aside and said. "Mr. Chairman, I have concluded my remarks."

Gregg used his gavel again while Judge Church sat down to applause, to that same restrained applause given Oldham.

"I have said the meeting would be opened to general discussion — " he began.

Immediately Chuck Cleaver was on his feet, heedless of the gavel. "My name is Charles Cleaver," he said, his voice sounding high as if forced through a choke. "I own a ranch next door to some land already leased." He swallowed and forced more words through. "They'll poison my creek. They'll poison my stock ponds and wells. They'll kill me with coal dust." He threw his arms out as though to ask help. "Don't you see? It's my ranch. It's my life. It's — it's the land."

Now a thicket of hands went up, and voices yelled for recognition. The chairman with his gavel finally restored order. He repeated, "I have said this meeting would be opened to general discussion." He pointed to his watch. "But it is getting quite late. The formal presentations took longer than planned for. Obviously we can't hear everyone tonight, or even a fraction of those who want to be heard. I declare this meeting adjourned, to be reconvened at a date that will be announced." He got to his feet.

There was muttering, but by one and twos and groups the

crowd began leaving. A few went to the desk to look at the strip-mining map. I put my tablet in my pocket, shrugged on my coat and left with the others.

At the opened outside doorway I was held up by a cluster of men. I heard someone say, "Fight." I pushed my way through.

On the front steps, half-lying down, was a man whose hand wiped a bleeding nose. He was Jope Jordan, a rancher. He was struggling to get up. On his feet, his hands locked into fists, Chuck Cleaver stood at the ready.

I yelled, "Hey, now!" trying for authority. "Take it easy. No more fighting, please."

Cleaver cast me a glance, his face working. He still talked in jerks. "He sold out. The son of a bitch sold out. Leased his land. It's next to mine and upstream." He glared at Jordan, who was getting to his feet. "That's right, you bastard. Stand up and take what you got coming."

I stepped between them and said, "That's enough. Cool it."

Jordan began wiping at his face with a bandana. There was fury in his face. "Next time," he told Cleaver, "carry a gun. I aim to kill you."

"Shit. You haven't the nerve. Sell up and get out, betray your neighbors, that's your size."

I had both of them under some control now. At least I thought so; I knew it when Cleaver let out a good-bye, "Son of a bitch," and let me lead him away.

The rest of the night was quiet.

❖❖❖ 7 ❖❖❖

THERE WAS LITTLE TO DO, off duty, in Midbury, unless you
wanted to cruise the one drag like a kid or kill time and yourself on a bar stool or play gin rummy or poker, little to do unless you had a wife and perhaps children or maybe belonged
to a lodge or shot pool.

Such pastimes held no steady appeal for me, and I had no
such involvements, and so it was that I was in the office early
the next afternoon when two men entered to talk to Charleston. I recognized Arthur, alias Oily, Oldham. He came forward
and offered his hand to the sheriff, who stood up for the offer-
ing. "Arthur Oldham of Energy Associates," he said. "I want
you to meet the president of our company, Mr. Ames." They
shook hands, too.

Charleston said, "My deputy, Jason Beard." After the for-
malities were over, I arranged chairs for the visitors and took a
seat at the side.

The two men were clothed in assurance and respectability,
adorned with geniality. They wore dark, three-piece suits with
neckties, their shoes were shined, their jackets and hats, which

I had hung on a rack, had never graced bargain counters.

In their presence I should have felt shabby. Sheriff Charleston didn't need to. He always wore a fresh-pressed white shirt, decorated now with a string tie. His frontier pants fit him. So did his indoor and matched jacket.

Oldham threw a questioning glance at me, to which Charleston replied, "Jason is entirely reliable."

"We are grateful for the time you are giving us," Ames said. "Grateful and pleased. Your reputation as a good officer is far-reaching."

Charleston didn't say, "Thanks." He didn't say anything. He just sat, listening.

"My company is facing some difficulties." With Oldham it had been "our" company. He wasn't the president. "As you know, we have been held up in our operations, held up unduly, all reasonable men will agree."

Oldham put in, "Pending approval. Waiting on red tape."

Charleston gave a bare nod.

Ames resumed, "They are costly, these delays. Dead time, we call it. We have machinery ready to go, men ready and eager to work, but no engine can turn and no man ply his trade. The men are restive, of course."

Charleston said, "They would be."

"They feel unwelcome, even in danger. In certain quarters they meet hostility. That's the ignorant cowboy element, of course."

"Your men will be protected," Charleston said. "And I am aware of the opposition to strip mining."

Oldham joined in again. "That's good. That assurance of protection. As for the opposition, it is misguided. It doesn't know or will not recognize the facts. I tried to explain that last night."

"Jason, here, heard you."

Oldham, his courtesy showing, turned to me. "And what did you think, Mr. Beard?"

"It was quite a discussion."

"I keep coming back to costs, unjustified costs," Ames said. "Unemployment insurance is running out for some of the men. For others it has already run out. It's barely enough to hold a crew together as it is. As a responsible employer, concerned with the welfare of our men, we supplement the insurance checks and in some cases support the men all on our own. But time goes on as the money goes out, and every day that an expensive machine stands idle constitutes a drain on our resources. It's an intolerable situation."

Charleston said, straight-faced as before, "I can see it would fret you."

Ames smiled. "I am happy that you get the picture, Mr. Charleston. I knew that you would understand and be sympathetic. That's all we can ask and all we do ask. Honest understanding."

"And meantime wait approval," Charleston said.

"I must tell you this," Ames said, leaning forward. "At the first hint of approval we start getting out coal. At the first hint of it, I repeat. Let the consequences be what they may."

Oldham supported him. "A thing started is a thing started. A thing done is a thing done. That's our thinking. The dust will settle."

Charleston looked at the ceiling, then back, and didn't speak.

"It seems we have a happy meeting of the minds," Ames said. "To go on, then. We support good government, Mr. Charleston. When a good man is in office, we want him to stay there. It's to our interest and everyone else's." He allowed time for his words to sink in.

Charleston answered, "I see." His manner suggested to me that he didn't like what he saw.

"Now," Ames went on, "I believe you have an election coming up?"

"November."

"Unless you stage an energetic campaign, unless you have the means for it, some unfit man, some whippersnapper, may be put in your place. Right?"

"It's possible."

The two men didn't see danger. They couldn't read his expression. It might have passed for serene but for the unrecognized glint in his eyes and the tightening of lines at his mouth.

"We wouldn't want that to happen," Ames went on. "No, sir, not that. To ensure against it, we offer substantial support. Substantial, I promise you. Enough and more than enough to return you to office. A contribution to the cause of good government." He waited for an answer and got it.

Charleston didn't raise his voice. He didn't need to. The words came clear and hard. "I've listened to you," he said. "Now I want you to listen to me." His eyes, as they fixed one man and another, put me in mind of glass caught by the sunlight. "If you try to jump the gun with your strip mining, if you proceed before final approval, if you gouge out one shovel of soil, I'll stop you."

It was like an unexpected fist in their faces. They fell back, dismayed, and bent forward, mad.

"For Christ's sake!" That was Oldham.

From Ames came, "The hell you will!"

Charleston held his ground.

Oldham found words. "It's not your say-so. It's up to the state and federal agencies."

"You bet your life it is," Ames said. "You're off the reservation, Charleston. It's not in your jurisdiction, not for one god-damn minute."

"The law is the law, and I'm a sworn officer of it, and that's it," Charleston told them.

Ames broke out, "You damn fathead. You won't listen to reason."

Charleston rose straight from his chair. "Neither will I be bought. Good day, gentlemen."

I let them get their own jackets and hats. They went out with mutters. Charleston muttered something himself. I couldn't quite hear it but it might have been, "Sons of bitches."

He was my man.

◆◆◆ 8 ◆◆◆

IT WAS MIDNIGHT, nearing the end of his shift, when Doolittle radioed me in the office.

"I'm at the Chicken Shack," he said. "A man's been shot
dead."

I asked, "Fight?"

"Nope. It was Pudge, the bartender."

"The dead man?"

"That's what I said."

"Who did it?"

"God knows. Shots came from outside."

"Shots?"

"Right. Someone was plunking the lights."

"Come again. What lights?"

"On the sign. The outside sign."

"Have you called Charleston?"

"I thought you better do that."

"I'll be along after I do."

Charleston answered on the first ring. I told him what I
knew.

"Go over there right away," he said. "I'll get hold of Doc Yak and Underwood. See you."

I snatched at the keys, ran out of the office, unhooked a police car and cranked up. The night was cold, colder because I had forgotten my coat. The Chicken Shack sign glowed ahead of me, some of the lights not working. It showed "Chi--en Sha-k."

I wondered whether I had heard shots while I drowsed in the office. It seemed to me I had and mixed them in a dream.

I ran up the porch steps and threw open the door. A half-dozen men were in the barroom, not drinking. They looked up, silent, as I entered. Doolittle was waiting in the forefront. He said, "Upstairs."

He led the way to the back of the place, and I followed him up a narrow, wood-splintered staircase. We went through a small bedroom, where I had to stoop but Doolittle didn't, because the ceiling slanted. It gave onto a similar front bedroom where a man lay on the floor and another sat hunched on the bed, his gaze fixed on the still figure.

"That's Pudge, and this here's his brother, Ves Eaton," Doolittle informed me.

Ves Eaton didn't look up. He was muttering to himself, "The dirty son of a bitch! The goddamn bastard!"

Glass from a shattered front window crunched under my feet as I stepped ahead. Pudge was dead all right. I knew so after I had lifted his head and felt of his wrist. A bullet had entered just under one eyebrow and come out at the top of his head. I saw splatters of blood and brains.

I straightened. "Doc Yak will be here in a minute. You haven't disturbed anything?"

Ves Eaton might not have heard me. Rage was in his face

66

and dry grief. He said, not to us, "Poor Pudge never hurt no one. What the hell? What the hell?"

"Nothing messed up that matters," Doolittle said.

"Hold on," I told Eaton and got out my notebook. "What's your full name?"

"I got all that," Doolittle put in. "It's Silvester Eaton. Pudge's first name is Vivian."

"Brothers?"

"Yep. And partners."

"No trouble between them?"

Eaton gave the first sign of attention. He said, "Goddamn you!"

"No trouble as I know of." The speaker was Doolittle again. "They were getting along. Then someone had to start popping the lights."

"And poor Pudge went to the window for a look-see and got himself shot," Eaton told us.

"Sure?"

"What does it look like for Christ's sake?"

"How come he wasn't tending bar?"

"Go shove your questions. All right. He tended bar mostly while I took care of the other stuff. But tonight I relieved him. That's the size of it. Oh, hell."

"And no one downstairs saw anything? Not Tim Reagan or Tony Coletti or anyone?"

"It happened fast," Doolittle said. "I ran outside, along with some others, when the lights got to popping. No one was in sight. Then Ves went upstairs and found his brother, fresh shot."

"Did he go alone?"

Eaton lifted his torn face to me. "You stinkin' snoop! Think I did it, huh? Killed my own brother?"

"Not necessarily. Why did you go upstairs?"

"To see could Pudge take over while I went out to look around. Investigate, you would say."

There was a tramping on the stairs and footsteps in the adjoining bedroom, and Charleston came in, followed by Doc Yak and Underwood. Charleston gave me a quick look, and I nodded, trying to tell him we had put the first questions.

Doc Yak went forward and bent over the body, his satchel by his side. "Plain to see," he said presently. "No need for more examination. Beyond help. That's him." He rose, "The goddamn luck of life. Crazy bastard son of a bitch." Death always offended Doc.

Eaton started up from the bed. "Who you talkin' about, quack?"

Doc pointed down at Pudge. "Not him. Not anybody. Just things. Now go soak your noodle."

Eaton subsided.

"What caliber gun, would you say?" Charleston asked.

"Big enough. I'm not a ballistics man. You want a ballistics man, go get yourself one," Doc said.

Underwood edged forward. "Can I take him?" He always seemed eager to make away with a body, perhaps to resume his study of baseball all the sooner.

Doc said to Charleston, "I can tell you one thing. The man who shot him down stood there right in front of the place."

"Couldn't be," Doolittle replied. "I or someone would have seen him."

"Blind fools, all of you, then. Look here, Charleston." He raised the dead man's head. "Bullet went in under the left eyebrow, as you can see, and came out the top of the head near the front. An angle shot, a sharp upward angle. Only a man right down below could have fired it."

68

Eaton had been listening, his face dark and drawn. "I ran out, too. There was no one there, no matter what shit you tell us."

"Everyone to his own shit," Doc said and picked up his bag.

"Can I take him now?" Underwood asked again.

"Goddamn it, yes," Doc told him. "I'll want to examine him later."

"All right, men," Charleston said. "Everybody out."

We filed down the steps, all but Felix Underwood. At the bottom two men waited with a litter. Charleston told them they could go on up.

Before we got to the bar Charleston asked Doolittle, "Did you get anything from these men?" He nodded toward the group ahead.

"All they knew, which wasn't anything. I know as much as anyone, and that's damn little."

"Enemies? Any mention of them?"

"Ves told me Pudge didn't have one single enemy, not to his certain knowledge."

"You talked to everyone, all the men present at the time?"

"All present and accounted for."

Charleston gave a quick nod of his head. "Nothing more here right now. Come along, both of you, please."

We drove the cars to the courthouse, hooked them into the electrical outlets and went on to the office. I was shivering.

Once we were seated, Doolittle and I told our stories. They added up to nothing much except for the plain fact of a death.

Charleston asked Doolittle, "You sure there wasn't anybody just outside as Doc Yak insisted?"

"If there was, he got out of sight damn quick." Doolittle scratched his head. "And we would have heard him shooting, I think. The way it was, I can't say I heard any shots at all, what with the talk and the juke box going full tilt. Then someone heard the light bulbs exploding or noticed the difference in the light cast outside. I don't know which. Anyhow, we were late catching on."

"Ves Eaton went upstairs alone, so you've told me. What about him as a suspect?"

Doolittle was shaking his head. "We would have heard that shot for sure. I looked around but didn't see any gun. Dead end, I'd say."

"Jase?"

"Ves Eaton's grief seemed honest enough. Likewise his anger. I don't think there's anything there."

"Were they about of a size, same approximate height?"

Doolittle answered, "Ves was a couple of inches taller."

"Still, he could have shot up from the hip. That would account for the slant of the bullet."

"I can't buy that," Doolittle said. "Who shoots that way, unless in danger and one hell of a hurry? Besides, Ves went up and clattered right down the stairs, howling and screeching like a tomcat. He wasn't out of sight more than a minute."

"There's another possibility," Charleston said slowly. He doodled with a pencil on an old envelope. He looked tired. He let us have time to think of the possibility.

The answer hit me just as Doolittle spoke. He said, "Ricochet."

Charleston nodded his agreement. "We'll have to see, if we can. That sign on the edge of the porch, I believe, is supported by steel rods that angle out from the building proper. A bullet, hitting one of them, would glance up. If that's the case, we'll find the rod scored."

Charleston yawned and got up. "All that's for tomorrow."

Doolittle suggested, "We could maybe find the bullet in the woodwork."

"If my guess is right, that battered piece of metal wouldn't help," Charleston replied. "Can both of you be here in the morning?"

We answered sure.

"We'll need your reports." Charleston sighed and regarded us almost in apology.

"I can't type," Doolittle said.

"Jase can."

The sheriff gave us good-night and went out.

I went to the typewriter and inserted paper while Doolittle sang to the old hymn, "Work for the day is coming."

"Got anything better to do?"

"I can dream up a few things, but, being highly responsible of late, I have to say no."

We finished sometime before dawn.

❖❖❖ 9 ❖❖❖

I SILENCED THE ALARM CLOCK after the first ring, hoping my mother hadn't heard it. I shook my head, trying to tell myself that I had slept long enough. Long enough? From 3:30 to 7 A.M.? A cat might have made out with that nap.

It was still dark, and my bones told me it was still cold. In a right world no one would have to get up in the dark. No one would have to shiver and shake.

I shaved and took a shower and threw some clothes over my goose pimples, thinking to slip quietly out of the house. But the kitchen light was on and the heat there turned up, and Mother was busy at the stove. I smelled frying bacon.

"This is ridiculous," I said. "You didn't have to get up."

"Omelet or scrambled, Jason? Quit fussing."

At the table I said to her inquiring look, "A man was killed last night. That's why I'm up."

"Killed! Who was it?"

"One of your foreigners, Pudge Eaton by name."

She sat down, holding a coffee cup, and said, "By one of his own kind, I suppose. Did you say shot?"

"I didn't, but he was."

"It doesn't sound like one of our people, killing a man."

"It's happened before."

"Very seldom. It's not characteristic. Jase, what's your hurry? Finish your breakfast."

"No time."

A dying half-moon hung in the west. In the east the stars shone. Another day with a cold sun, and the sun dogs showing, but what would Pudge Eaton care?

Charleston and Doolittle were already in the office. The radiators were clanging, not to great effect. I started to take off my coat.

"Not now, Jase," Charleston said. "You and Ike go and examine those metal supports, struts I guess you call them, that hold up the sign at the Chicken Shack. Borrow a ladder from the county shops. Report pronto, huh? You, Jase, I mean. Ike, see if you can rout out one of the Shack's customers and bring him in."

"Not Ves Eaton?"

"Try Tim Reagan. Afterwards we'll canvass the neighborhood. Go on."

A sleepy shop worker let us have the ladder, an eight-foot aluminum extension, though he didn't much want to. I held the ladder through the open window at the side of the car while Doolittle drove. In the pursuit of justice, what's a frostbitten hand and arm? The sun was peeping up, cheerless, as if it could bring no hope to the world.

The Chicken Shack stood forsaken, its blinds drawn, the broken window boarded up; the dispenser of joy juice had quit dispensing.

We slanted the ladder, extended, against the porch. Doolittle swarmed up it almost before it was in place. He hadn't gone far until he called out, "Eureka! Seek and ye shall find."

Satisfied, he came down, and I took my turn. The support was scored all right, the support that angled up toward the boarded window. There was the scratch just above the edge of the porch, then a deeper impression, then another scratch, the brightness of metal showing through the black covering. I could believe that the bullet, striking it, had been deflected into the window. I could believe it, though no one can predict the way of a ricochet.

Back on the ground I said, "That looks like it. Just what we figured. I mean Charleston figured."

"So it does, Doctor Watson, so it does. Now I must go cozen Tim Reagan."

"I don't know if I can cozen the ladder alone."

We solved that problem by lowering the back windows of the car and sliding the ladder across. I said as I left, "Send out the dog and the brandy if I don't show up by tomorrow."

I drove the car to the county shops, delivered the ladder, rolled up the car windows and went back to the sheriff's office.

Old Doc Yak was inside with Charleston. At Charleston's inquiring look I said, "Good guess."

Doc Yak hadn't sat down. He was saying, "Damn you, Charleston! You play hell with my practice."

"I was under the impression, Doctor," Charleston said, his voice and face bland, "that your importance to this office increased your prestige."

"Prestige, hell! What's prestige to an empty purse?"

"I shall call your services to this office to the attention of the county commissioners."

"Awfully kind of you." Doc threw himself in a chair. He handled his body as he handled a car, headlong and to hell with the consequences, which he seemed never to think about, anyhow.

I sat down.

"Now that you've got back your sunny disposition, tell us what you've found," Charleston said.

"I assume you are talking about one Pudge Eaton."

"Come off it, Doc."

"It's the damndest bullet wound I ever saw." Doc settled back. "Either he had a whiff of buckshot or he had a cast-iron skull."

"Go on."

"The bullet fractured, you might assume, but the entrance hole wasn't round. It was ragged. I probed and brought out a couple of small metal pieces besides one a little larger. It would have done the business itself, but the boss piece went clear through the skull, as you know. It'll be lodged in the building somewhere."

Charleston nodded and said, "Inside job possibly?"

"You ask some fool questions. Inside job, hell! Since when did window glass shatter in the direction of the hit? Ask something else."

"We ask a lot of dumb questions, thinking of the possibility of a put-up job, of a collaborator, though that's probably a cold trail." Charleston leaned forward. "Here's another one for you. A direct hit would have made a starred hole in the glass. It wouldn't be likely to shatter it. That's how it figures. What do you say?"

"I don't say."

"It was a ricochet, Doc."

"So be it then. You're the detective. I'm just a sawbones. I leave it to you." Doc rose from his chair. "Now, if ever you want me, call me up, night or day. You know my number, but I wish to God you didn't." Abruptly he smiled. "Forget the fool part, Chick. Sometimes you're fairly bright."

He went out the door, almost colliding with Doolittle and Tim Reagan. Reagan sat down as Charleston waved to a chair. Doolittle kept on his feet.

"It's good of you to come, Mr. Reagan," Charleston said.

Reagan sat on the edge of his chair, chin out, unsmiling. "Just because Ike asked me to. Let's cut out the shit."

"All right. We want to know how and why Pudge Eaton died. Did he have any enemies that you know of?"

"He died because some son of a bitch shot him. You maybe lost a marble, Mac?"

Doolittle broke in. "Quit playing the dumb Irishman," he said to Reagan. "You're not doing yourself or anybody else any good. Answer what's asked. And Sheriff Charleston's name isn't Mac."

I expected trouble then. There wasn't any. Reagan said only, "Oh, hell, Ike. Okay."

"I ask again, did Pudge Eaton have any known enemies?"

"Christ, we all got enemies. The whole town's our enemy. Too good for the likes of us. We came here to work, no harm done, and what with one thing and another we're kept off our jobs. And who in this fuckin' town will so much as speak to us? Enemies, huh!"

"Particular enemies? One particular enemy?"

"None that I know of. Hell, Pudge was nice to everybody."

"I understand there was some disagreement at the hearing the other night? About whether to strip mine?"

"Just one guy."

"Chuck Cleaver?"

"If that's his name."

"Do you have any reason to suspect him?"

"That country bum! He didn't even know Pudge."

"What about Pudge's brother?"

"What about him?"

"Suspect him?"

"Jesus Christ, no! Don't talk shit to me."

"All right. Who owed money? Anyone in deep to the Chicken Shack?"

"We all run a tab. Pay it when we get our checks. What else don't you know?"

"Thank you, Mr. Reagan," Charleston said evenly. "As you can see, we're only skirting edges. I see no reason to bother you again."

Reagan let Doolittle show him to the door.

With only the three of us present, Charleston asked, "So you found the marks?"

I answered, "One of the supports was scuffed up, the one right under the window. Ike and I both examined it."

"It figures," Charleston said, more to himself than to us. "The lights were the target. One shot went high."

"So it's not murder." Doolittle had his hand on his chin and was only half-asking. "Accidental death."

"But still a homicide." Charleston paused and considered. "What was the purpose in shooting out the lights? Mere harassment? By whom and why? Reagan has no idea. That's all we got out of him. No idea, except everybody in town." He got up and went to the window, which he couldn't see out of, frosted as it was. "Maybe we better keep the ricochet business under our hats. Only the man with the gun knows about that, and he might be happy if we chase off in other directions. Let him think we don't know." He turned. "You two question the neighborhood. That's next."

Dismissed, Doolittle and I left the office.

We drove to the edge of what I had come to think of as Skid Row, though I had read that the word was "road," which derived from the trails that skidded logs made in the timber country. Yet neither term was appropriate. The same went for Shanty Town. Call it Trailer Town then. Some of the mobile homes sat on blocks, some on their own wheels, as did most of the campers. TV masts made a thin forest above them.

We left the car and agreed to start at the ends of the row and work toward the middle. Being the senior officer, so to speak, I said I'd walk to the far end while he set to work close by. Rank has its drawbacks.

Walking, drawn in against the still bite of the cold, I counted the dwellings, the temporary and movable abodes of a class of people, of a growing kind of civilization strange to me. Would the whole country come to that, moving from fugitive rich pickings to new ones, as gold miners had done when their claims played out? No permanent residences then, no place to call home except a wheeled box? No picket fences? No lawn or garden to tend? No sense of being part of a known and loved landscape? Onward, roll on to the next shabby payroll.

Not so shabby, though. Not in money. The cars that I saw parked beside or behind these places were expensive and looked new. All that was missing — no, not all but a big part — was permanence.

A dirt road, its ruts frozen, ran in front of these homes. I counted fifteen as I stumbled along. I stopped at the fifteenth, a mobile job on blocks, and knocked at the door. A dog let out a wild barking, sounding above the din of TV. A woman opened the door, a small woman in slacks who looked shel-lacked. Transient or not, I thought, she wouldn't let herself be caught without make-up.

"Good morning," I said. "I'm from the sheriff's office. May I ask you a few questions?"

"For God's sake, come in then," she answered. "Every time I open the door this place turns into an icebox."

I entered. She closed the door and went to sit on a turn-out bench. She motioned toward the one easy chair. "Have a seat."

"I won't be long," I told her, staying on my feet. The dog, a poodle, had quit barking and was trying to make love to me. The place was cramped, God knew, but tidy.

"You've heard about the death, Pudge Eaton's death?"

She turned the TV down while I warded the dog off.

"Poor Pudge," she answered. "Yes, I've heard. You, pup, stop being a nuisance."

"You know he was shot then. We think the rifleman may have been fairly close by."

"No one had it in for Pudge. He wasn't too smart, but he was nice."

"The question is did you hear anything last night or see anyone? Anything or anyone suspicious?"

"Not a sound, unless you count the TV, and not a soul."

"Are you sure? Did you take the dog for a walk? Or did your husband?"

"My husband was soaking it up at the Chicken Shack, or I guess he was if his credit's any good there now. He told me about the shooting."

"I'd like to talk to him."

"Find him, then. He went out this morning, probably for more of that juice. Damn such a life!"

"In his absence you must have walked the dog?"

"Now that you speak of it, I did, and now that you speak of

it, I caught a glimpse of a boy. He was just turning out of my sight."

"A boy?"

"He was real small, anyhow. Short and thin."

"Was he carrying anything? A gun maybe?"

She thought hard. "There was something in his hand, I think, something like a stick, a walking stick. I couldn't swear. It was so cold that my eyes started melting, if you get what I mean."

"But you didn't hear any shots, any sounds?"

"I don't remember any. I had the music way up." She made a little despairing gesture. Her eyes were melting again, not from cold, and the melt smudged her cheeks with mascara. I thought of a small and dirty-faced child. "Just me and the god-damn TV, day in and day out, and the nights lonesome, too." Her voice came out in a cry. "Christ, man, what's a girl to do? What's she to do?"

I felt like going over and patting her. I wished for someone who could kiss her tears away, mascara and all. "Carry on, I guess," I mumbled.

"Chin up and all that crap," she said, lifting her head as she wiped her eyes.

"May I have your name?"

"Yes. I'm Marie Coletti. If you're a drinking man, you've met my husband."

"I'm not much of a one, but I have. Thanks for answering my questions." I put my hand on the doorknob.

She rose and stood, looking like girlhood forsaken. She asked, "Must you go?"

The words weren't an invitation. They weren't a pass if my mind told me right. Marie Coletti just didn't want to be left alone. At least that's what I felt sure of.

I said, "I'm working. I'm sorry," and left her.

The TV was blaring again as I walked to the next unfixed abode.

I didn't get anything more, if, for a fact, I'd got anything from her. I talked to neat women and slobs. I entered clean places and dirty ones. I met kids and more dogs and a couple of men who weren't drowning their sorrows. No one heard anything. No one saw anything. Those who weren't at the Chicken Shack had kept themselves closed against the cold, their TV sets blaring.

About halfway down the row Doolittle and I came together. I asked him, "Any fish?"

"One old gal might have seen a man, a tall man, gangly-like, she said. He wasn't carrying anything that she saw."

"Case closed," I told him. "My girl saw a small boy."

❖❖❖ 10 ❖❖❖

It was a little past noon when we met, and we parked in front of the Commercial Cafe, went in and had sandwiches and coffee. Other customers, what few there were, came by to ask about the killing. Ike kept answering for us both. "We don't know anything that you don't. Maybe not as much." Which wasn't the whole truth but near enough.

When the curious were not around, I asked Ike, "What about Tony Coletti?"

"He's a crafty bird. Watch out for him."

"Boozer?"

"He doesn't belong to the temperance union."

"What about his credit?"

"I wouldn't want to go on his note. What you sniffing at?"

"Possibilities," I answered. "Pipe dreams, maybe."

We drove back to the office, wishing the car heater would warm up, and went in to report.

Charleston was alone. As we entered, he crumpled up a sheet of paper that I saw he had been making notes on, saying, "So much for that." He put his hands to his head and drew them down over his face as if to smooth out the thought wrinkles.

Doolittle told him what he had found out, which wasn't anything, and I told him what I had, which added up to nothing plus.

But maybe a little bit more. "Tony Coletti likes his liquor. That's what his wife led me to believe. Likes a lot of it."

Charleston asked, "Uh-huh?"

"Suppose he had run up a big bill at the Chicken Shack and couldn't pay off and the Eatons had said nix to more credit?"

To me Doolittle said, "So that's what you were sniffing at."

Charleston tapped on his desk, not in impatience but to the steps of his thought. "Was Coletti present in the Shack at the time of the shooting?"

"Give me one more chance, please, Mr. Sheriff," Doolittle said to him. "I'll make a deputy yet. No, he wasn't there, but I never gave thought to it."

I added, "Neither did I till just now. Not even when I was pointing his way. One more chance for me, too, if you please." I was lying a little for Doolittle's sake.

"Maybe something there," Charleston said, musing. "Just maybe. Resentment. Outrage. Sense of injustice. Tit for tat. Could be, I suppose."

"Especially if Coletti got hold of another bottle somehow," I said.

"Doolittle, you can find out about the credit. That comes later, though." Charleston's gaze went from one of us to the other. "You both look pretty saddle-sore."

Doolittle spoke. "The mail must go through, sir. I'll climb a fresh horse."

Charleston said after the briefest of smiles, "I'm afraid you'll have to." He went on to explain. "Tad Frazier's got his hands

83

full. Three break-ins at summer cabins. I'm going to talk to Chuck Cleaver and want Jase along. He knows Cleaver better than I do and stands more chance to get something out of him, if anything's there. You take over the office, Ike, until I get back. I'll relieve you then. Jase, you'll have time for a nap when we return, but try to report back about eight o'clock. At midnight I'll come back on. All right?"

"I'm not that tuckered," I said, but Charleston just answered, "Come along, Jase."

We got into his old Special, which he had bought and maintained himself for special purposes, though I could see nothing so special ahead of us.

We rolled along through a winter world. Now and then, right and left, we saw three or four horses and small bunches of cows, trying to fuel themselves on the sparse and frozen grass. Save for them we were alone, two silent men and a piece of machinery, life in a lifeless expanse, the open fields rolling away to hills and the hills to mountains scant-patched with snow. The sun, more than halfway through its journey, glared coldly, an enemy now, a partner of frost. Even with my heavy socks and boots and the heater going full tilt, my feet felt the creeping cold through the floorboards.

Yet my country, I thought, my proper place, my point of outlook on men and things. Love could keep loving even though it got the cold shoulder. A jack rabbit, white as the expected but unfallen snow, leaped from the side of the road, ran ahead of us and jumped back in the borrow pit. I felt better for seeing it.

In one of the few conversations we had, I said, "Why Cleaver? What might he tell us?"

"He's the only lead we have."

"Except Coletti."

"Yes. Possibly. Possibly."

We turned off the highway, went over a cattle guard and started through a long field, at the end of which Cleaver's house stood under a plume of chimney smoke. A bunch of cows were in the field. Seeing us, they started following, their muzzles frosted. Anything on wheels gave a promise of hay. I had to shoo them off when I opened a gate. They stood in slow disappointment when we left them.

Cleaver was coming from the barn as we pulled up at the house. His face, tight with cold, showed no surprise and no welcome. Coming closer, he sidled along an old farm truck, equipped in back with the usual toolbox.

I rolled down a window and said, "Howdy, Chuck. Got time to talk for a minute?"

"I s'pose. But if we got to talk, for Christ's sake come in the house."

He showed us in. I caught a glimpse of Mrs. Cleaver through the kitchen door. The door eased closed, as if men and their affairs were no rightful concern of women. Cleaver said we could sit down if we wanted to.

The living room held overstuffed furniture — three chairs and a sofa through which the circles of springs showed and now and then the bare end of a spring. The carpet was worn down to threads. A round-bellied wood stove was fighting the cold and losing. A border collie, an old bitch, lay close to the stove. That breed of dog is not unfriendly but not demonstrative, either. She lifted her head and put it back down. We kept our wraps on.

"It didn't take two of you," Cleaver said.

Charleston answered, "We just wanted to talk."

"You could have told me by phone."

"Told you what, Chuck?"

"That that pissant neighbor of mine filed a charge. You know damn well I belted him one, leasing his land and to hell with me. What is it? Assault and battery?"

"Nothing like that," Charleston told him. "There's no charge."

"Then what?"

Charleston nodded for me to take over.

"A man was killed last night, Chuck," I said. "The bartender at the Chicken Shack. Had you heard?"

"We listen to the news."

"Apparently the man who did it was shooting out the lights and fired one shot high."

"That's the way it sounded."

"All right, Chuck. We have to investigate. We're questioning everybody, everybody who might have any motive at all."

"Go question them then. I'm out."

"Would you tell us where you were at the time of the shooting?"

"When was that?"

"Didn't the radio tell you?"

"If it did, I forgot."

"At eleven o'clock or close to it."

"And where was I, huh?"

"Yes."

"Right in my little bed. Rancher's hours, not sheriff's."

"Could someone confirm your whereabouts? Witnesses, I mean?"

"Sure. Everyone watches me sleep."

Charleston took a deep breath and blew it out. "For all that we know, you could have done it."

Cleaver's jaws ridged at the open suggestion. In that outdoor face were weather and years and work and hardship. No wonder that sometimes he went on a binge. Through his teeth he said, "For what goddamn fool reason would I do that?"

"You don't like strip miners."

"Damn right I don't. But why the hell shoot out lights? Why shoot a barkeep that I never saw? What would that get me? Tell me that, Mr. High Sheriff."

"I don't know."

"If I shoot, it will be at one of the bigwigs, you can bet your ass on that. Or maybe at one of those big-shovel jockeys or smart-ass grease monkeys. Jesus Christ, where's your brains?"

Charleston answered mildly, "I guess I left them at home. But we have to ask around."

"Fart around, then." Cleaver got up. "Good-bye."

He slammed out the door, leaving me, at least, with nothing much to chew on.

On the way back to town Charleston said, "Well?"

"He used to have some fun in him."

"Not now. He's on edge."

"I guess in his fix anyone would be. You know, strip mining and then us landing on him."

Charleston eased the car past a poky truck. "What may a man do, when he feels the sands start slipping under his feet?"

"I don't quite get it, but he's not licked yet."

Charleston said, "Not yet," and fell silent.

I asked to be let off at the Bar Star.

He looked at me from the side of his eye, and I said, "Don't worry. I'll get a nap."

Bob Studebaker had just one customer, a homesteader named Samuelson. I sat at the bar and ordered a drink.

Pouring it, Studebaker said, "I didn't hardly recognize you, stranger."

"Been busy. How's Gunnar?"

"Fine. Best damn dog a man ever had, even if he does eat me out of house and home. Want to see him?"

"Sure."

He went to the back of the place and let the dog in. Samuelson took one look at the dog, gulped his drink and started edging for the door.

"He won't hurt you. Be a good dog now, Gunnar."

Samuelson took his leave, his eyes on Gunnar until he got to the door. Opened, it let in a puff of white that faded into a draft. I put my hand out for the dog to sniff. He must have remembered me, for he licked my hand with a tongue as big as a steak.

I asked Studebaker, "Do you know a man by the name of Coletti? Tony Coletti?"

"He's been in a few times. You know I don't cater to them offbeats, but what the hell? This is a public place."

"Is he into you for anything?"

"He's got a big thirst, but I've never seen him what you call drunk."

"Is he?"

"Well, now, just for a couple of bottles. He'll pay off. He's done it before. Always made good."

"When was the last time he got a bottle?"

"You're goddamn curious, Jase, but it was just last night. No, come to think of it, this morning. A man forgets. Don't you worry. I'll get my money."

He didn't quite ask me why I was curious, and I didn't tell him, just saying, "You know your customers."

I walked home through the gathering dark, slept for three hours, gobbled my supper under Mother's anxious eyes and headed for the office.

"You're early," Charleston said after a glance at the wall clock.

"But fresh as a daisy."

"Picked when?" He took a moment to size me up, then went on. "Doolittle's checking with Ves Eaton before going to bed."

"About Coletti? About his credit?"

"That would seem to be the idea."

"You're awful tired, Mr. Charleston."

"Tired and cranky," he admitted with a small smile. "Something on your chest, Jase?"

"Coletti owes the Bar Star. Studebaker said for a couple of bottles, but it could be more. He got one this morning. Credit good there, so far."

His head made a small up-and-down movement. It wasn't affirmative. It wasn't negative. It was brooding. He rose and said, "I'll relieve you at midnight. Be at ease if you can."

Left alone, I shuffled through what facts we had. They were few and led nowhere. We knew a man had been killed by ricochet by another man who had been shooting at lamp bulbs. We knew of the social division between townspeople and newcomers. I knew Coletti had been boozing it up. And where was the hunch in any of that? I drowsed and reflected and reflected and drowsed and came out by the same door as in I went, as old Omar had said. Doolittle wasn't the only one who could employ classical references.

At ten-thirty Mrs. Carson called from the switchboard. "There's a woman wants to talk to you. She sounds hysterical."

"Put her on."

"Sheriff," a high voice told me, "please come! Come quick or it's murder!"

"Hold on. What's your name?"

"Kate Reagan. Mrs. Tim Reagan. I live — "

"I know where you live. Who's being threatened?"

"Threatened? You mean being beat up. Marie Coletti."

"I know where she lives. Where's your husband?"

"I can't find him."

"Who's beating her up?"

"Her husband. That Tony." The voice rose higher. "Don't ask questions for God's sake. Just come!"

I stopped at the switchboard only long enough to tell Mrs. Carson to roust out Doolittle and tell him to come to the Coletti place. Then I ran out, yanked the cord to the engine heater and burned rubber getting away.

A woman stood cold and nervous outside the Coletti place. I said, "Mrs. Reagan?"

"Yes. In there. In there! I was thrown out."

The lights were on in the Coletti trailer. I heard a woman crying out. I threw open the door.

There was Marie, lying slumped on the fold-out bench. There was Coletti standing over her, fist raised. He moved at the sound of my entrance. I could see then that Marie's face was bruised and bleeding. She had her hands clamped over her stomach.

Coletti said, "Get out!"

I took a step forward.

"Family business. Get out!"

"No! No!" the girl said between her bleeding lips.

"You shut up, you bitch!"

"It's public business now. Move away from her."

Through the open door, from over my shoulder, came a hoarse voice. "Coletti! You bitch-born wop."

It was Tim Reagan behind me. He tried to push past. Behind him I caught a glimpse of a police car pulling up. That would be Doolittle.

"Wop, huh?" Coletti was snarling. "All right, you mick, you two-timer." He stabbed a finger toward Marie. "You and her both."

"Stand back, Reagan," I told him. "Police business."

Turning back, I said, "Come along, Coletti. You're under arrest."

"For man and wife business? Go screw yourself. She's a born whiner. Two-timer, too. She even talks to pigs, so I'm told. I been teaching her better."

I felt Reagan pushing against me. A glance showed me Doolittle and Mrs. Reagan, crowding close.

"Come along."

From the tiny kitchen table Coletti snatched a slicing knife. He pointed it at me. "Sure. Take me. Take me and my knife."

In his hard glare, in his sure movements, I saw the hard craze of alcohol and the muscular control it sometimes gives to a man.

"For Christ's sake, stand back," I yelled at those behind me. "Give me room."

I had to give Reagan an elbow. He was saying, "I knowed that girl since she was a minnow. Let me take him, god-damnit."

"Stand back!"

I hate men who abuse women. Rage rose in me and came to a boil. Blind rage.

I moved toward Coletti. He started feinting with the knife, crouching, knife held low in knife-fighter's fashion.

I stepped almost into the thrust of the blade and kicked him in the face. He went down. I tramped on his knife hand, sending the knife skittering. He was moaning. I yanked him to his feet. I hit him full in the face with my right. He went down again, not moaning. I yanked at him again and felt a hard hand on my shoulder. Doolittle's voice said, "That's enough, Jase. Cool it."

"Stay out of this!"

"You're an officer, Jase. Remember that. Don't louse things up."

Rising, I felt the rage seeping out of me. It left entirely when I looked into Doolittle's eyes. There was troubled concern there.

"Thanks," I said. "You got handcuffs?"

"Right here."

"Cuff him behind his back."

Coletti didn't protest. He was only half-conscious.

"What about Marie?" Reagan wanted to know.

"I want to go home. Back to Boston," the girl said in a thin voice.

"In time," I told her. "Right now you're coming home with me."

"How's that?" Reagan asked bristling.

"No need to worry. I promise that."

Doolittle got Coletti to his feet and said to Reagan, "Hold him up, will you?" He stepped over and picked up the knife.

"Marie, do you want to come home with me? My mother's there. She'll take care of you."

She swayed to her feet, still clutching her stomach. "Anywhere," she said, her tone frail. "Anywhere but here."

"Ike, take Coletti to the jail. You can handle him?"

Reagan said, "I'll go along, just in case."

I half-carried Marie to the car. She didn't weigh much more than a child, and, like a trusting child, she let me seat her.

I went around to the driver's side, and there was Reagan again. "She's not a two-timer, goddamn it," he said. "Don't get ideas."

Before I closed the door I told him, "Sometime you must meet my mother."

I rang the front door of our house, thinking to prepare Mother a little. She opened the door, her eyes big on the picture we made.

"This girl's hurt, Mother. Needs care."

Her gaze went to Marie. "Oh, you poor dear. Come in out of the cold. In the kitchen. There's hot water on the stove. Please come in, dear. I can call a doctor."

I helped Marie to a chair in the kitchen. One of her eyes was almost closed. There was blood on her chin. I could tell her stomach still hurt. "You'll be all right now," I told her.

Mother answered for her. "Of course you'll be all right."

The girl said, "Please send me home."

"I'm off again," I informed Mother.

"When you're better, of course you'll go home," Mother was saying.

I slipped out the door. I didn't need to give my mother instructions. She would take charge. I knew that and gave thanks.

Charleston was alone, waiting to relieve me. I started on my story of the night, but he interrupted me. "Doolittle told me. He's in back with Doc Yak. If you want to add anything, it can wait."

"One immediate thing, Mr. Charleston. It may take that girl a week to recover. I wouldn't want Coletti bothering her or my mother. I hope he's kept behind bars for a while."

He answered, "Don't worry," and at the same time the back door of the office opened, letting in Doc Yak and Doolittle.

Doc Yak glared at me. "I want to make one observation. When you arrest a man, you sure as hell arrest him. Broken nose. Two teeth gone. Face all bunged up. Bump on the head. Do you have to knock the shit out of a man before bringing him in?"

Doolittle was quick to answer for me. "It was all self-defense. We got witnesses. Pure self-defense. Look at that knife slice in Jase's coat." I hadn't noticed it. Neither had anyone else until he spoke.

"Doc," I said, "you're on your high horse. Please come down. My mother's got a hurt girl on her hands. She needs you right away."

Charleston nodded. "She just called, trying to find you."

"Well, now, your mother," Doc said. "That's a different story. Fine woman. How she birthed such a brat as you, Jase, I can't figure. Anyhow, I'm long gone." He gave me a smile as he left. Doc's degree of liking showed itself in abuse.

"One or two things I didn't get in, chief," Doolittle said. "Ves Eaton said he didn't know a thing about Coletti's credit. Pudge always took care of accounts, mostly keeping them in his head. And I didn't see any rifle in Coletti's place. I'll look more tomorrow."

"All right, go, both of you," Charleston ordered. "Get some sleep."

I went home then, stopping just once at the Bar Star for what I told myself was an earned drink.

Walking on in the still and frozen night, in the ringing bowl of the valley, that night, for the first time, I heard the howling of wolves.

◈◈◈ **11** ◈◈◈

OVER AN EARLY DINNER I asked Mother, "Where's Marie? Isn't she up to a meal?"

"She's much better. No internal pain at all. It's just that she doesn't want to be seen with her face all discolored. I don't blame her. She's a good girl, Jase."

"One of the foreigners, just the same."

"Don't frown on her because of that. She can't help it, and good is where you find it."

"Yes, Mother."

"Another thing, Jase. She's worried about her dog."

"Dog! Oh, for Lord's sake, I forgot about it. It wasn't in sight last night."

"She says it always hid during any unpleasantness, under a chair or bed or some place." She turned to face me, her gaze searching. "You must have run into a lot of unpleasantness last night."

"Enough to spook a pup, I suppose."

"How did you get that tear in your coat?"

"What am I, a suspect or something?" I asked. I hated to

dodge her honest questions, but if I didn't she'd worry her head off. "I learned something. Don't try to crawl through a barbed-wire fence with one of those bulky coats on."

She murmured, "Hmm," only half believing. "Anyhow, it's mended."

"Thanks, Mother. By the way did you happen to hear howling last night?"

"I didn't want to mention it because you'd just laugh at me. All right, though. It woke me up. I kept the light on. What was it, Jase?"

"Just dogs. That stands to reason."

"It didn't sound like dogs to me. More like wild animals."

I did laugh then and said, "Scaredy-cat. Hear noises miles away, and you get the wind up."

"Just the same, I didn't like it."

She sniffed, dismissing that subject. I refused the offer of more coffee. "Marie wants to go home. Boston, it is," she said. Her mind was bouncing around like my own. "She says her family will send money if she gets word to them. They never did approve of the marriage."

"Tell her to phone them."

"It's so expensive, and she has no money."

"Say it's by courtesy of the sheriff's office."

At the door, after I had bundled up, she said, "If you see Doc Yak, please thank him. He came right away, and he's such a nice man."

I said, "Yes, Mother," again.

I had time to drop in at the Bar Star. A half-dozen customers were there, and old Tom Curtis was saying, "They was wolves, all right. Hell, I know wolves. First time in forty-five years I ever heard them howl around here. Scared the bejesus out of my woman."

I shook my head when Studebaker asked me, "What'll you have?"

Francis Fournier, a half-breed, picked up the subject when Curtis left off. In our town we didn't have blacks or Mexicans to exercise our superiority on. We had Indians and part-bloods. But Fournier owned a little property and maintained a bank balance and so had the credentials for brotherhood. "From Canada," he was saying. "That's where they come from. Starved out up there, and frozen out, and so they come south. Like the big white owl. Arctic, they call them. I seen two yesterday."

"Time we organized a wolf hunt," Bodie Dunn put in. "That's if the women will let us out at night."

"If we could just sic them wolves on the miners and then shoot the wolves, that would be a good cleanup," Curtis said.

"Serve 'em right, too," Dunn added. "Throwin' them bricks through old Willsie's window. That gets me."

The talk turned to Pudge Eaton's death. I had heard enough, and my time was up. I went out and walked to the office.

At the switchboard Blanche Burton was fixing her face in preparation for going off shift, though I could hardly see why. The present climate was not conducive to socializing. But a lonely woman couldn't afford to be careless.

"You have a little visitor, Jase," she said. She must not have heard last night's howling.

"He, she or it?"

"Go see for yourself."

When I opened the inner door, Marie's little poodle barked and came bouncing. On the floor were a saucer of water and what remained of a meal. Doolittle, seated, smiled and said, "He was crying his head off. Brave officer to the rescue."

I patted the poodle, asking, "What's your name, pup?"

Doolittle told me, "Bipsie. Hell of a name for a he dog."

The dog went to a corner and lay down, exhausted from his show of affection. I asked, "Has Charleston seen it yet?"

"Not yet. Ought to be back any minute. That's the word from the board."

I called Mother to tell her Marie's dog was safe and sound. While we waited, I asked Doolittle, "How do you like your job?"

"Fine. Just fine."

"Mr. Charleston is satisfied. I guess he told you. And you're okay by me."

Doolittle put a hand to his trim mustache, his eyes on the floor. "Jase, if you asked me what I'd done in my life, I'd have to say damn near everything rough. I've run trap lines in Alaska, herded sheep in Nevada, followed the harvest, signed on as a roughneck in the Oklahoma oil fields, worked with cattle and hell knows what else. Once I worked the rodeo circuit until I got too old and those broncs were driving my guts down into my pants. I called any place home. But none of those jobs was permanent and nothing I did important. Wasted time, except that I always read whatever I could lay my hands on. Yep, a wasteland, that was my life. But now —"

He raised his eyes to me and said almost shyly, "To tell the truth, I'm getting a taste for respectability."

Before I could answer, Charleston came in. Bipsie, revived, gave him a welcome. Doolittle told him whose dog it was and explained its presence. "And, chief," he went on, "there's no sign of a gun in Coletti's place. I went through it, top to bottom, side to side and underneath."

Charleston sat down. "How did you get in?"

"I heard the dog howling."

98

I interrupted with, "He wasn't the only thing howling last night."

Charleston glanced at me, said only, "So I noticed," and turned back to Doolittle. "So you broke in?"

"Now, chief, you ought to know me better than that. The door was unlocked."

"Doubtless. Doubtless," Charleston said. A smile touched one corner of his mouth. "Otherwise you might have needed a warrant."

"Maybe not, with the dog howling so pitiful. You wouldn't want me to face a charge of cruelty to animals, would you?"

"Heaven forbid. So Coletti didn't have a gun in the house?"

"Nary a one. What's more, Tim Reagan told me firearms weren't their ticket, not his or the gang's. Come trouble, they relied on shillelaghs and bicycle chains."

"And knives?"

"That was only Coletti."

The switchboard called. Charleston answered and said, "Have the chief come on in."

City Police Chief Leo Bandy came through the door. He was a small round man with a large round face. With what seemed an effort he was holding his chest out. He ignored Doolittle and me and spoke directly to Charleston. "This has got to stop. I'm telling you that, Charleston."

"Sit down, Chief Bandy. I'm listening."

"Be damned if I sit down. I just come with a message, that's all."

"What's got to stop?"

"You taking jurisdiction where it belongs to me. A man killed and a girl beat up right in the city limits. That's my territory."

"Nobody kept you out."

"And nobody notified me, not you or anybody else. God-damnit, everybody calls you. What you think we got a city force for?"

Charleston raised one eyebrow. "Force?"

"Right now, it's just me and one officer, but by God we're here."

"So." Charleston drew out the word. He made a doodle on a piece of scrap paper. "Suppose, then, we turn over to you all that we have and resign from the cases?"

"Now I didn't say that." Some of the bluster had gone out of Bandy. "You're too far in to get out, and we're too far out to get in. I was pointin' to the future, that's all."

"Message received," Charleston said, staring Bandy down. "Here's the answer. This office is responsible to all the tax-payers of the county, those within the city limits included. They pay taxes, too. We will continue to meet our responsi-bilities with or without you, in the county and in the city. Do I make myself plain?"

"You heard what I said," Bandy answered and turned to-ward the door. His chest had resumed its normal position in his belly.

"I heard you. Thanks and good-bye." Charleston watched the door until it closed, then said, "Pisswillie." It was his word for trifling vexations. "Maybe we can get down to business now."

I spoke what was first in my mind. "Those wolves howling last night?"

Charleston said slowly, "What sounded like wolves."

"Begging your pardon," Doolittle interjected, "they were wolf howls sure enough. I've heard many a one, from singles and packs. What's more, on a still Arctic night their voices will carry six miles."

"I don't doubt that carrying quality," Charleston said and didn't say more.

I wanted to add that the howling I had heard didn't strike me as the tail end of sound, but Charleston dismissed wolves with a thrust of his hand. "Coletti ought to be alert enough now, no matter what Doc shot into him. Go see, will you, Ike? Bring him in then."

After a minute or two Coletti came in the back door, guided by Doolittle. His eyes took in Charleston and me through swollen lids, and he said, "Sons of bitches."

He might have been a prizefighter the next morning after fifteen losing rounds. Bruises put his face out of shape. They were turning from red to purple to yellow and green. His broken nose, packed, showed white at the nostrils. Of necessity he breathed through his mouth, and, when he spoke, his tongue moved behind a gap in his teeth. For an instant I felt guilty, but only for that long.

"Sit down, Mr. Coletti," Charleston said. "We have some questions to ask."

"Hey, that's my dog," Coletti said. "Come here, you Bipsie."

The dog crept, cowering, under a chair, and Charleston remarked, "Obviously he knows you. Sit down."

Coletti seated himself shakily. If the sedative had worn off, the hangover hadn't. He told Charleston, "I want a lawyer."

"Any time, but I must tell you that the testimony of witnesses will be more damning than anything you may admit. I am speaking of last night."

"So what about it?"

"First, let's deal with the night of Pudge Eaton's death. Where were you at the time?"

"Oh, no! You can't hang that on me. Son of a bitch if you can."

"Perhaps not, but you weren't at the Chicken Shack. We know that. So where were you?"

"I don't have to tell you."

"No, you don't. Of course you wouldn't want to if you were taking pot shots at the lights. What was the reason for that? Had the Eatons closed off your credit?"

Coletti said, "I need a drink." He did, too, with the shakes he had.

"The sooner you answer, the sooner you'll have your drink. I promise you that. Now where were you when Pudge Eaton was shot?"

"If you got to know, I'll tell you. I was laying up with Erma. She's one of the Chicken Shack girls, and she's got her own little house. You can ask her. She'll clear me."

"We will," Charleston said and sighed. "So much for that."

"You lettin' me go?"

"I'm afraid not, Coletti."

"Why not?"

"Because of the charges against you."

"I can get someone to put up bond."

"We must wait to see how your wife gets along."

Coletti sucked a breath through the gap in his teeth. "Gets along? What the hell you mean? Gets along?"

"Just what I said. Gets along." Almost idly he added, "I suppose you know you can't post bond on a murder charge?"

The breath caught in Coletti's throat, then wheezed in and out, faster and faster. He said to himself, his eyes fixed on the floor, "Oh, sweet Jesus! Not that. With just a slap or two." His head jerked up, yanked by some mistreated nerve. He strangled out, "Whiskey!" His voice was weaker than his need.

Charleston took a half pint from a desk drawer, handed it

to Doolittle and said, "Let him have it. Take him back. Better nurse that flask along, Coletti. It's the last you'll get."

As the back door closed, I said to Charleston, "There's more than one kind of a kick in the face."

"And ways to keep a dirty bird in a cage."

He took his leave, saying before he went out, "Tad Frazier will relieve you along about midnight."

Walking home in the clamped cold that night, with Bipsie trotting along behind me, I heard again the wild voices of wolves.

❖❖❖ 12 ❖❖❖

BLANCHE BURTON was sending a message. "You there, Ike? Hear me? Good. Drive out the Titusville road, to the McDonald mailbox if necessary. Young Ronald started for town three hours ago and promised to call home but hasn't been heard from. His folks think he may be stalled. Go see. Mr. Charleston's orders. Fine. That's it, honey."

I stood by the switchboard, listening until she signed off. "I declare," she said, "he's even nicer than you are."

"They say he's pure hell when his dander's up."

She sniffed, unbelieving, and answered, "Trashy people do wag their tongues."

I went into the inner office. Charleston was saying "Goodbye" into the telephone. He greeted me, lighted one of his thin cigars and through the smoke said, "Crazy hours we're all keeping. No organization. Things get in the way of it. Frazier's out on a fire alarm. Maybe nothing, but he'll get there ahead of the county fire truck and see can he help. Doolittle's busy, and as for you, God knows what hours you've been keeping."

"I'm not kicking. Anything new about Pudge?"

"No time to pry." He drew on the cigar. "How's Mrs. Coletti?"

"Much better. She got in touch with her parents. They're sending money."

"Good. When is she planning to leave?"

"She's talking about day after tomorrow."

He studied the smoke he had blown out. "It's a shame. The office hasn't done what it should."

I asked, "What's that?"

"You've never been on winter duty before? No. Of course you haven't. It's been our habit in bad weather for one of us to tour the back roads of the county, making sure no one is in trouble. That's part of the duties of this office."

It wasn't really. It was a self-imposed duty, and good politics besides, though I had never known politics to influence his operations.

"Right now," he continued, "I'm a little worried about old Ernest Linderman. Know him?" I didn't. "Lives off the Petroleum road, fifteen miles or so away. Then there's old Mr. and Mrs. Whitney, not so far off. Better check on them, Jase, but wait." He made a quick sketch on a piece of paper. "Here's a map."

"Any others out that way?" I asked him.

"What others?"

"I was thinking, well, don't the Duttons live somewhere around there?"

"It's the old ones who may need help."

"The way I hear it, that grandpa can't be young."

"He's got young help." Slowly Charleston leaned back and smiled. "Do I detect something there, Jase?"

"I just thought —"

"All right. All right, boy. I'll put the Duttons on the map, but their place is out of the way. Make that your last visit, if you make it at all."

He gave me the map. I didn't see how I could go wrong.

"And, Jase," he added, "take along that old .30-30 carbine on the chance you see a wolf."

"I heard other hunters were going out."

"Yes. And shoot themselves full of liquor and maybe lead."

"Anyhow, they're hunting wolves, not miners." Speaking, he made a face.

I rose to go, but he stopped me by saying, "One thing first. Go talk to that woman — what's her name? Erma — that Coletti says he was with at the time of the shooting."

"Doolittle could do it better than I. He knows all those people."

"But it's you that has to be satisfied."

"Not you?" I asked.

He took a little puff on his cigar and, breathing out, said, "No stone unturned. So turn it, Jase. You could be right."

I took the carbine, saw that shells were in the magazine and said so long.

Tim Reagan was filling in as bartender at the Chicken Shack. Four men sat toward the rear end of the bar. The two women I had seen before were seated at a table. The men eyed me and eyed Reagan as he walked toward me. I supposed they hoped for trouble. They turned back to their own affairs, however, when Reagan said, "How are you, Jase?"

"Hunting information as usual."

"My well's been pumped dry."

"Not quite, Tim. I want to know who's Erma."

His thumb flicked toward the table, and he answered, "The tall one."

"Send the ladies a drink, please."

There were two extra chairs at the table, and I took one and said, "Howdy, ladies."

One, the short one, said to the other, "He wants it for nothing. All cops do."

The men at the bar weren't paying any attention. They were talking about wolves.

"I believe you're wrong, Pearl," the tall one answered. "I think I smell trouble." She was dark and would have been good-looking except for paint and wear and tear. It seemed to me her eyes were sad, as if she saw the end of the road and knew it was the wrong one, to boot. But it was too late to take the road not taken, Mr. Frost.

Tim brought over drinks for them, and I paid. They didn't thank me.

"Erma," I said, "I want to know where you were at the time Pudge was shot."

She batted her eyes. "Now when was that? Let me think. Oh, yes, the night he was shot. I was attending to business."

"With whom?"

"Hear that, Pearl? Oh, my! 'With whom.'"

"Make it who with."

She drew herself up, playing the grande dame. "I do not reveal the names of my clients. Professional secrets. They're privileged."

I said, "I could run you in any time."

"It wouldn't be the first time, tough guy. Is the food good at your jail?"

"Bread and water. For variation, water and bread."

She let a smile, not professional, touch her face. "He makes jokes, Pearl."

"I'm laughing my head off," Pearl said. She reminded me of a bunny that unfortunately had turned into a plump rabbit.

"I'm all fun," I said. "Only right now I want an answer to my question. Where were you?"

"At my home until after midnight. That's where."

"With company?"

"I'm crazy about company."

I said, "Quit sparring. Tell the truth."

"I haven't lied yet."

"You haven't said anything, either." I softened my tone and explained, "I'm not here to trap you. What you tell me can't get you into trouble, unless you fired the gun, which is a crazy suspicion to me. I'm asking you please, Erma. Plain please."

Now her gaze met mine and didn't shift away. "It's been a long time since anyone said please to me."

"Please."

"He knows how to get his way, Pearl," she said, her eyes still on mine. "All right, Mr. Law, please. I was at my home from nine-thirty until after midnight. Who was with me? That fine gentleman, Mr. Tony Coletti. He was too drunk to perform. That's polite talk, so you will understand. But he tried and tried and kept trying. He nipped at a bottle, too, between tries. Maybe that raised his ambition, but it didn't raise anything else. And all the time he didn't have a dime in his pockets. That's the sad story."

"Would you swear to what you've just told me, about his presence, not his performance?"

"If I have to." Her arm jerked suddenly, spilling some of her drink. "But who would believe me? What good is my word? Not worth a damn."

I motioned to Tim to refill the glasses.

"It is with me, Erma," I said and got up, leaving money on the table. Her breath said thanks.

So scratch one Tony Coletti, I thought as I left. Too bad. Too damn bad. He deserved worse.

The car engine was slow to fire, though it hadn't had time to get really cold. What was needed was a new battery. What was needed was a maintenance man. At last I got the car going, headed out on the road toward Petroleum. I kept an eye out for wolves. It seemed, when I opened the window a crack, that I could hear them howling.

The night was blind black. Not a star shone. Not the moon. In warmer weather, with the clouds low, a man might expect snow. Not now, though. Not as cold as it was. My headlights tunneled through the dark. They shone lonesome, the only lights in the world.

Five miles or so out of town I saw a gleam on the road ahead. It grew into two, and I dimmed and pulled to the side. The other car stopped beside mine. A window rolled down and revealed Bodie Dunn. He asked, "Huntin' wolves like us, Jase?"

"I'm ready for them. Any luck?"

Bodie held a flask out the window. "Have a drink. Join the party."

From inside the car came other voices, hearty with whiskey.

"No thanks, Bodie. Not on duty. What's your score?"

Bodie took a pull at the flask. "We heard 'em, that's for sure. But score? Maybe we wounded one. We couldn't tell."

From inside the car a laughing voice yelled, "Ghost wolves. We been layin' ghosts. Gimme that bottle, Bodie."

As I was about to roll up my window, Bodie said, "We'll get some yet."

I drove away, hoping ghosts were all they would lay, or had laid.

I found Ernest Linderman's place without trouble, though I had mislaid the map. A door opened as I approached it, and a rusty voice said, "Come in, stranger. Warm your butt. Hey, ain't you Bill Beard's young 'un?"

I gave him a yes and entered. "I'm a deputy sheriff now. Just cruising around."

A straight-backed chair stood by a stove made out of an oil drum. An Aladdin lamp gave what light there was. Either rural electrification hadn't reached that far or Linderman couldn't afford the cost of a line. Close by a rocking chair a collie lay, dozing. It opened one eye and wagged its tail. There were a plank table and a couple of chairs to the right of the door, and a very small wood range under the rear window. Pots and frying pans hung from a wall.

"Tell Chick — he's a good man — not to worry about me," Linderman was saying. His voice came through the phlegm of disuse. "No, sir. I get along." He poured me a cup of coffee without asking. It tasted of long boiling.

"Set, boy," he said easing himself into the rocker. "Like I was saying, I get along, though I been too busy fightin' the cold to get to town. My chickens froze their combs in spite of a coal-oil heater I keep in the hen house. My two cows come close to freezin' their tits off and would have if I hadn't rigged a blanket sling for 'em. I'm near short of wood, split wood, I mean, so I got to go out and chop blocks. Cold work, I tell you. More coffee?"

"This is fine, thank you."

There was an old arch-fronted radio on a stand table. I wondered if he ever used it. The wooden floor was scrubbed clean.

Catching me in my survey, Linderman said, "Not bad for a bachelor, huh? I been batchin' it for ten years now, ever since my wife died. No young 'uns, though we tried hard enough. But I don't get lonesome. I'm a tough old bird."

I could believe him. His hands and face — and the rest of him for all I knew — might have been made out of old harness leather. He had a sharp face and good eyes, bright blue in their leathery wrinkles.

"Any wolves been howling around here?" I asked.

"Wolves don't worry me, except I aim to keep 'em away from my stock. Lots of scare stories about wolves, but hell, you got to show me a case where they ever tackled a man. That's what I was tellin' the Whitneys. They came by once, kind of skittish, after hearin' the howling sort of faint-like."

"They were all right?"

"And left feelin' better."

"Anything you need? Anything we can do for you?"

"Not a Lord's thing. Not a Lord's thing. But wait, now. Don't go. It's nice to have someone to talk to."

"Talk to" was right, I thought. I doubted I had said more than a dozen words.

"A man alone gets to thinkin'," he said, settling back. "Now some would say a man gets to be a slave to things, specially live things that he shelters and feeds. I don't see it that way. It's good to have critters depending on you. Gives you a worth-while feeling. Take my dog. He knows he can count on me. Same with the cows and chickens. I'm the ace-high boss, and a boss sees to his own. Right? Take away responsibility, and what have you got? Nothin'. You might say I'm depen-dent on dependence, if you got to bobtail it. That suits me. See?"

He fed the fire in the boiler and sat down again. "We get along, me and my stock. We get along, come hell or high water. Cozy, we are. Who needs help or has to have company?

No, no, boy, I wasn't talkin' about you. Visit a while longer, can't you?"

I made my excuses, leaving a man alone and was again alone myself.

This time the quirky engine started with the first revolution, though the headlights seemed feeble. Funny. The battery should have gained strength as the car ran. Driving, I blamed myself for not inquiring about the way to the Whitney's house. I braked to a halt and searched my pockets for the map Charleston had drawn. No map. Damn the cumbersome wraps a man had to wear in this weather.

I came to a fork in the road and, trying to remember, took the right-hand trail. It was no more than that, just wheel ruts, unfenced. Farther on, my lights picked up a hulk to the left. The hulk grew into a truck with a man standing beside it. I veered left and rolled to a stop. The man had a rifle in his hands. Before I recognized him, he called out, "Dowse those lights!"

It was Chuck Cleaver, standing dark and hard to identify beside his dark truck. After I had greeted him, he asked, "You huntin' wolves?"

"Looking for them, anyway."

"You ought to know better. Huntin' with lights on. Scare all the wolves back to Canada."

"How can you see them in the dark?"

"By waitin' for my eyes to adjust. That's how."

"Howling again tonight?"

"Tonight and near every night lately. Got to get rid of them. Calvin' time's comin', and they would play hell."

I asked him where the Whitneys lived.

"You took a wrong turn. Go back to the forks to the other

road. You'll have to look sharp for a turnoff. That's to your right, five miles or so. What's wrong with them?"

"Nothing I know of. The sheriff wants me to say hello."

"They was all right last week."

I said, "Good hunting."

Before I could roll away, he answered, "I'm rackin' up. Wolves see car lights, even on dim, they skeedaddle."

Look sharp, I thought as I turned around. Sure, look sharp with bum headlights. I came to the forks, and another trail angled in. It couldn't be the turnoff. I hadn't traveled that far.

The headlights faded. They shrank to mere blinks. The engine sputtered and came to life and died. The starter clicked. That was all.

Nothing to do but radio the office. Yes, Mr. Charleston, I know I'm a green officer, green as grass and about to freeze my tail off. It would serve me right, that's true enough, but I'll try to do better.

My mistakes ran in my mind. I should have made sure about the car, and I hadn't. I had lost the map and lost my way. I forgot to ask directions from Linderman. Anything else? Anything more in the way of incompetence?

I tried to raise the office, tried and tried again. No answer and no wonder, not if you had sense enough to know the radio worked off the car battery. Add another item to the amateur list.

I took a flashlight from the jockey box, decided the carbine was just an encumbrance and locked the car. I stepped away from it and tried to find bearings. The outline of a mountain would have helped, or the shape of a butte, but the dark hid all profiles. There was nothing but dark, no star shine or moon shine or break in the black.

Roads had to lead somewhere, I told myself, pushing aside the thought of dead ends. I would follow the road to hell or the pole, one or other, for there was no turning back, not at this distance from Linderman's. I flicked on the flashlight. Its beam was dim. Tonight was the night for new batteries. I turned it off for emergency use.

I followed the road more by foot feel than sight. I stumbled and fell down and got up and went stumbling on.

I tried to shove from my mind that ours was a big county — 2,294 square miles, the assessor had told me once. Not flat miles but square miles of plains, benches, foothills and mountains. Probably no man knew every county and wagon road, every coulee and gulch, every gouge the streams had made in the life of the land.

The cold was getting to me. Cold was a creeping thing. It began with the fingers and toes, the nose and the cheeks, and moved in toward the center of life, toward the furnace of the heart, not to be satisfied until it got there. I slapped my arms around myself, I tramped my feet and tried to wiggle my toes. My fingers had lost feeling. It was a wonder they worked.

A man's mind plays tricks on him when he is lost in the dark. He imagines wolves on his trail, waiting for him to collapse. He imagines them ahead of him and around him, jaws dripping. He expects the dark to take hungry shape. I did and tried to shake the thoughts from me. I sang and yelled and whistled in my graveyard. And once I beamed the flashlight on my back trail. There weren't any wolves there.

A wild snort and thrashing sounded almost in my face, and a shape arose, blacker than black. It was darkness solidified. It was black night in person.

It wasn't, though. It was an old horse, as startled as I was.

The flashlight told me that. I moved around him, saying, "Whoa, boy," and heard his hooves following me. Better to be followed by an old horse than a wolf pack.

The flash found the road for me and found a telephone pole at the side. Roads might lead to dead ends. Telephone lines didn't, that was for sure.

So step and step and stumble and stumble while frost worked into the bones. Another telephone pole. Good. Excellent. How far did the damn line run? Too far for help? A race, then. A plodding race between me and the cold. Distance uncertain. The old horse was following along.

A line kept singing in my head, *I am weary of days and hours.* Yes, brother, weary of everything but sleep. Not quite, though. The cold was still a presence. I could feel it. It had brought tears to my eyes and frozen the tears, and my eyes were sticky. I rubbed them roughly. A light seemed to show far ahead. I rubbed them again. It was a light or my fancy or a crystal frozen on an eyelash. I squinted and fell down again and got up, my feet as heavy as anvils, and went on.

I stumbled up a couple of steps and knocked at a door. A female opened it, and her voice said, "Good Lord, come in! I never saw such a sight." A hand seized my arm. "Come along."

Something in me led me to say, "The ice man cometh." It was relief or bravado or both. I wasn't sure my stiff face let me smile.

"Out of your head to boot," she said, "making jokes while the bell tolls."

I felt a dim delight at that response. And I felt more than that. Even through frosted lids I recognized her. Here she was. Now we had met. I almost forgot I was cold.

She was taking off my down coat. She pulled off my gloves

and pushed me into a chair before a stove. It was an old round stove with isinglass windows. She fed it with blocks of wood.

"Now," she said, looking me over. She wore a pair of jeans and a plaid shirt.

I said, "My name's —" but she interrupted me. "Introductions later. Frostbite first."

She took a basin from a cabinet and poured water in it from a kettle that was purring on an electric stove. She found a towel in a drawer and wet it in the basin. "Hold this to your face," she told me, handing me the towel, "hot as you can bear it. No, not ice or snow for frostbite. That's for old wives. Heat's the thing. Left cheek, please. It's the white one. Put that hand in the water. Two fingers white there. Your feet next."

I managed to put in, "My name's Jason Beard. I'm a deputy sheriff."

From behind me a voice, strangled with years, said, "Law or no law, keep your hands off my daughter." I couldn't squirm far enough to make out the speaker.

"Grandpa," the girl answered, "I hate to tell you to shut up but shut up. And I'm not your daughter."

"I had a daughter once." The old voice mumbled and went silent.

The girl took the basin and towel from me. "Can you get off your boots? Oh, here now, I'll do it. You'll never get them unlaced."

She was stooping. Her fingers were nimble. I felt mortified but knew that at least there were no holes in my socks, Mother being Mother. She drew out a second basin, filled it with water and said, "Dip your feet. Just dip for a while. You don't want to scald them. Our name is Dutton, in case you were wondering."

"I thought so."

She disappeared into what I supposed was a pantry and came out with a jelly glass one-third full. "Drink it," she said. It was bourbon. "What made you think you knew who we were?"

"Ike Doolittle."

I took a swallow of my drink. We were in a sort of combined living room and kitchen or, say, just a kitchen, for in ranch houses the kitchen is where you live. The furniture I saw looked old but comfortable.

"Ike," the old voice said. "Sure, Ike. I know. He's the one that got fresh with you. Right?"

"No. He didn't. You just thought so." The girl turned her head and said over my shoulder, her voice gentle, "It's your bedtime, Grandpa. Please go ahead now. Don't forget your medicine."

I put the basin down and squirmed in my chair. Grandpa was seated in a rocker. He got up nimbly, considering his age. "Have we had supper, Anita?"

"Yes, Grandpa. Won't you go on now?"

He gave me a grin with a mouth the years had fined down. He said, "Bright and early in the morning, Doolittle." Then he mumbled, "Oh, oh," as if he had caught himself in a mistake, and disappeared.

Anita said, "You must excuse him."

"I do, of course."

"Tell me, how is Ike?"

"Fine. He's a deputy sheriff, like me."

"He was a good man."

"And still is."

From the room the old man had entered, music swelled

117

out, loud enough to please the deafened ears of teen-agers.

Anita went to the door, knocked and said, "Please turn it down, Grandfather. You'll get a headache."

I set the basin aside and began putting on my socks and boots. The music faded.

The girl came back and sat by the fire, not speaking except to say, "Thawed out? Sure?"

"Only tingles left. I meant to ask you, have you heard wolves howling around?"

"Yes. Sometimes close, but they haven't done any harm. They excite Grandfather, though. Then he forgets."

She put more wood in the stove and sat down again. "I'm glad Ike's doing all right. He was a big help here until Grandfather fired him. I simply couldn't change his mind. For once it was fixed. He's the guardian of my morals, you know."

As if she had entered my mind, she went on, "I just can't put him in a rest home. He's been good to me."

It struck me all at once that the girl looked tired. The lines of fatigue and worry showed themselves in her young face. I was prompted to say, "How do you manage alone?"

"As best I can, that's all. Sometimes I want to give up, what with cows to feed and chickens to be looked after and the house to keep and meals to prepare."

"And Grandpa?"

"There's the garden in summer, too."

"And Grandpa?"

"Please," she said. Her eyes met mine. They were honest eyes, as honest as a silver dollar, as honest as one before it was made out of copper and junk and shrank to a dime in value. The beginning of tears showed in them. "I'm custodian, house-keeper, cook, stock tender, gardener and roundup rider." She brushed at her eyes. "Forget it. I'm pitying myself."

"Are you looking for help?"

"Who's to help? We can't pay very much. That's one thing. But we eat well; that's another. In one of his better moments Grandfather bought a deep freeze that we couldn't afford. Then, because I let them hunt the place, some hunters gave me a deer, all dressed out and cut up. I raised some turkeys last summer and some garden stuff. All that is frozen or canned now, and we do keep a flock of chickens and get a few eggs in spite of the weather." A smile erased the worry lines in her face. "How am I doing? You want a job?"

"It's a temptation."

"No perks." She looked a little roguish. "Remember Grandpa."

"I might know a man," I told her.

"A good one?"

"A little thick in the head." I was thinking of a character named Omar Test. "But he's energetic enough and can follow directions. No threat to your morals, either."

"Are you serious?"

"I wouldn't kid you."

"Can you find out?"

"I can."

"And would you?"

"I'll call you tomorrow morning. Phone working?"

"It was earlier."

"I've got to call Ike and tell him to rescue me."

"You've been rescued once." She was smiling.

"And now I don't want to be, but still —"

She showed me where the phone was, and I called the office. Mrs. Carson said she would get word to Doolittle by radio. I assured her he knew where the Dutton place was.

Anita made coffee, and for the better part of an hour we

talked of this and that, making conversation but something else, too.

Then a car showed up, and Ike knocked at the door. She greeted him warmly. He refused coffee, saying he had work to do. I heard the old man moving around.

At the door she shook hands with me. She had a small, strong hand, roughened by work.

"Tomorrow," she said.

I said, "Tomorrow."

In the cruiser Ike said, faking authority, "Report, please."

"The car conked out. The battery just got weaker and weaker."

Ike had the dash lights on, and I could see his face clearly as he turned and said, "Generator went flooey." The face smiled slyly. "But your own generator seems to be working full tilt."

❖❖❖ 13 ❖❖❖

I ROLLED OUT OF BED at eight o'clock, feeling frisky though I'd had little sleep, feeling frisky in spite of chilblains that would bother me more when I warmed up after being cold again. I shaved and bathed and got into clean clothes.

When I entered the kitchen, the dog, Bipsie, pranced to me for a head rub. Mother and Marie Coletti were seated at the table, eating hot cakes. Mother said, "Goodness sake, Jase, you're 'way early and all dressed up."

"Busy day ahead."

Mother rose and went to the stove and began ladling batter into the skillet. "Marie has made reservations for tomorrow," she told me.

"So soon?" I said. "One of us will drive you to the city."

"I hate to ask that," Marie said. "I've put you out enough as it is. I don't know how I'll ever repay you." Only a fading streak or two showed where her bruises had been. She wore less make-up than usual. An improvement, I thought. She was a cute girl, one showing good courage now, and, if she broke down, a man would feel a wanting to comfort her. Yet she would never have the western look, the look of sun and wind and of distance in her eyes.

"You just hush about that," Mother said to her. "It all evens up. We've been glad to have you. Don't just stand there, Jase. Sit down. These will be cooked in a minute." She began turning the hot cakes.

"I'll be ready," Marie was assuring us. "I've got my things from the trailer house." Her hand went to the dog and her eyes dropped to him. "I'm afraid I have to ask one more favor."

"Ask away."

"It's Bipsie. I simply can't push him on my family." Her gaze lifted to me. "Would it be too much? Could you find a good home for him?"

"He's a nice little pet," Mother said, putting a plate before me. "I'm sure any number of people would be glad to have him. Don't you think so, Jase?"

"Of course. Any number of people." I knew the way the wind blew, but I didn't smile. Let them work their little conspiracy. "I'll ask around."

"You must be sure they're the right people," Mother said.

"Come to think of it," I said, trying to speak as if the thought had just entered my mind, "I guess we could keep him. You're too much alone, Mother."

"Do you really think so, Jase?"

Marie put in, "I don't want you to, just to be nice."

"That's settled then," I said, giving them their women's victory without letting on that I knew all along. It pleased them and didn't displease me. The idea was so good it hadn't needed their strategy.

I ate bacon and two helpings of hot cakes, drank my coffee and made my excuses.

Omar Test lived alone in a shack on the south end of town.

For want of a car I walked there and knocked on the flimsy door. It opened after a while and revealed Test. He had on a ragged outdoor coat.

"Hello, Mr. Beard," he said, blinking his eyes. "You got a chore for me or something? Want to come in? I haven't built up the fire yet."

Entering, I thought he must have had to sleep in the coat. The room was as cold as a frozen-food locker. Our breaths made clouds in it. It held a rumpled bed, a chest of drawers, a mirror and a sagging chair. That was about all save for a cheap, sheet-iron stove. The place smelled clean enough, and Test looked fairly tidy in spite of uncombed hair and that old coat.

I said, "Want a job, Omar?"

"Sure do. Jobs been mighty sceerce."

"It's on a ranch."

"That don't matter to me. I savvy cows pretty good."

"The food will be good, and you'll have a warm place to sleep."

"Hunkydory, then."

"I must tell you that the pay won't be high."

"It never was, Mr. Beard."

He didn't speak in complaint. He spoke a fact. He accepted himself and his place without analysis. I felt a sudden surge of sympathy. He was an unassuming cipher. He always would be, but ciphers had their uses, not just in mathematics.

"And your boss will be a woman."

"Bosses is bosses. You know me. Just show me what to do and I'll do 'er."

"I know that, Omar. I suppose you'll want to tidy up some before going on the job?"

"Mr. Bob Studebaker, he lets me use that bath tub in back

of the bar next door to that big dog he has. I swamp out for him when he needs it."

"How are you fixed for an outfit? That coat's worn pretty thin. And how about heavy gloves?"

"I been gettin' along for years now."

"But I know you. You'll want to look nice."

"I got good boots. The preacher, he gave 'em to me. Bought 'em too small for hisself, and they raised corns on his toes."

"I got a good idea, Omar. Why don't you go to the Corral, buy a down coat and some warm gloves or mitts? Charge them to me. I'll see it's all right."

His dull, gentle gaze held a look of puzzlement. "Why you want to do that, Mr. Beard? It ain't Christmas or anything."

"Just say I want to. I'll trust you to pay me back when you can."

"Well, gee." He was looking at the floor.

"Can you be ready to go at two o'clock, say?"

"Nothin' to hold me back."

"I'll let you know if the time doesn't work out."

"I'll be settin' right here."

"I suppose you'll need a few things. A new toothbrush, maybe, razor blades, that kind of stuff."

He fumbled in his pocket and brought out a fifty-cent piece. "I'll just do without them things until payday."

I pressed a five-dollar bill on him. "No need to wait, Omar."

He looked down at the bill. "All right, I guess. Gee, be all right if I got myself barbered?"

"Sure. Just don't get drunk, Omar."

His face expressed what indignation it could. "You know I never been drunk in all my born days."

"That's why I said it. A joke, Omar. Remember, two o'clock."

I went to the one outside pay telephone in our town and called Anita Dutton. "I've found you a man," I told her.

"Already? How's your frostbite?"

"Smarting a little. I haven't paid much attention."

"How could you and find help for me so soon?"

"No sweat. He'll be ready at two o'clock. Can you drive in to get him?"

"Gosh, let me see. Well, I think so. I think I could leave Grandfather with Mr. Linderman."

"Do that as quick as you can. It would be better for me if you arrived at about noon."

"I see. You have to work?"

"Not that soon. I was hoping we could go to lunch."

She hesitated before saying, "That would be nice. I might be a little late, though."

"Just come along, please."

I walked to the Corral, told them I would stand good for what Test purchased, and from there called the office, hoping Mr. Charleston was there.

"Don't you ever sleep?" he asked. His tone seemed blunt. He might be thinking about the car I had had to abandon.

"I'm sorry about that cruiser," I answered. "I played dumbbell there."

"If that's what's keeping you up, forget it. A deputy has a right to think the cars are in shape."

"Thanks, but all the same I was stupid. Could I put off towing it in until the middle of the afternoon?"

"No, Jase, you can't."

"No?"

My question brought a small chuckle. "The reason you can't is that Frazier and Doolittle are on their way out there now. Nothing exciting here. Go get some rest."

I didn't need rest. I needed something to occupy my time. Anything. So at last I trudged to the office. Mrs. Vail was on the board. Because of my hours I had seen her only a time or two. She had a face like a camel and a shape to suit it and a brain like an erratic computer.

"Hello, Now and Then," she said. "I heard the brave deputy landed in clover after a treacherous time."

"I heard Ike Doolittle talks too much."

"He confides in those he can trust."

"And he trusts everybody."

She laughed. "You're borrowing from the story about the girl who limited her love to her friends."

"Yeah, and didn't have an enemy in town. You can do better than that."

"Here's maybe better. If you want to see Mr. Charleston, you better make time. He's about to go out."

Charleston was already on his feet when I entered. "Fine way to rest," he said.

"But I haven't told you about Coletti. I don't know where my mind's been."

"I won't guess," he said, smiling. That damn Doolittle! "But, yes, Coletti and that woman, Erma by name."

"She gave him a complete alibi, and I believed her."

"I'm not surprised."

"And another thing. Marie Coletti has made reservations for tomorrow. I can drive her to the city. On my own time."

He thought for a moment, pacing, his hands behind his back. "I'm afraid I'll want you around. Doolittle can chauffeur her. Show up a little early tomorrow if you can." He went out then.

I sat for a while. We were a long way from finding out who shot Pudge Eaton. I didn't want to think about that. I didn't want to think about wolves or strip mining or Coletti or Marie. So I didn't. Not much. I just sat there until noon.

Where to meet Anita? I hadn't mentioned a place. Neither would I recognize her car, never having identified it. Some datemaker! I walked the main drag, the seven blocks of it, watching for traffic, and returned, watching. I did the same thing once more. Then, chilled, I went to the office, and there she was, chatting with Mrs. Vail.

"Hi and welcome," I said. "Seems you two have met."

"I've been giving this pretty girl the lowdown on you, Jase." Mrs. Vail regarded us with the expectant, rather lubricious look that older women are likely to wear in the presence of a young couple.

"From what I've just heard, I must have been out of my mind, asking for you," Anita said.

"Please don't come to your senses then," I answered. "And don't accept at face value what Mrs. Vail says. She won the liar's contest last year and is trying for it again. Right, Mrs. Vail?"

"No fun in truth except for cops." The phone rang. "Run along, you two."

The Jackson Hotel was in one of its hopeful fits of improvement. The dining room had been redecorated and, so the advertisement said, a new chef employed. I took Anita there for lunch. The Commercial Cafe would have been as private as a political convention. The tablecloths were white, the napkins cloth and, as I found later, the menus new. I hung up Anita's wraps and my own. We had a choice of tables, improvement not having met its just reward, at least not yet.

I chose a table away from the windows through which the cold crept. She wanted a shrimp cocktail and soup. I ordered a cheese omelet. I guessed neither of us thought it quite decorous to give our appetites full rein. She told me she didn't want a cocktail. Neither, for that matter, did I. I didn't need one.

Cold-weather clothing gave the appearance of bulk and heft to all wearers. Now, with her coat hung up, her heavy gloves removed, Anita looked small but still sturdy. She wore a gray woolen suit and a white blouse with a touch of red at the throat. What's more, the suit had a skirt, not pants. The skirt was not the best of bad-weather protection, but it struck me as more becoming, though she could have worn pants without the plump ladies' appearance of defiance in front and apology behind.

Once we had ordered, I asked, "How's your grandfather?"

"Rounded up and safe with Mr. Linderman, but let's not talk about him. What have you been doing?"

"Finding you a hired man, waiting for you to appear and thinking about a case."

"Besides suffering chilblains. I suppose the case is that bartender?"

The waitress brought our food and we began on it.

"That's the case," I said. "No clues. We know he was shot. That's all."

"I hate guns. I hid the only one at the ranch."

"You might need it, for wolves or something."

"Then I can find it. Tell me about my new helper."

"I like him. He's not smart, but he works. Tell him what to do and, as he says, he'll do 'er. You'll have to arrange about wages. He'll be more than reasonable."

"You haven't told me his name."

"Omar Test."

"Not Tent?"

"No relation to the Tent Maker, and, besides, he doesn't drink."

We grinned at each other, pleased with shared knowledge. Her teeth were as white and even as a dentist's dream.

We chatted along without purpose, except the prime and unspoken purpose of getting better acquainted.

Over coffee she asked, "When do I pick the man up?"

I consulted my watch. "I hate to tell you he's probably ready now."

"Hadn't we better go, then?"

"After you answer one question. May I come to see you?"

"Not if you're afraid of Grandfather." Her eyes were full of mischief.

I said, "I'll just show him my badge."

We drove to Omar's shack in Anita's car. He opened the door when he saw us pull up. He looked quite presentable. I made them acquainted. Omar got in the back seat. As we rolled away, he said, "I hope it's all right, Mr. Beard. This new cap —"

"Sure. Sure," I interrupted. "Everything's fine."

Anita looked at me with suspicion but didn't say anything. I asked her to let me off at home and told her the way.

A wave of a gloved hand was the last I saw of her that day.

❖❖❖ 14 ❖❖❖

IKE DOOLITTLE CAME BY THE HOUSE at noon to pick up Marie and her baggage. Mother wasn't satisfied to say goodbye to her in the house. She put a coat on over her apron and followed us out to the car, with me carrying three light bags. She and Marie embraced, almost tearfully, and Marie even gave me a kiss.

As Doolittle was stowing away the last of the luggage, Tim Reagan showed up. I supposed Doolittle had told him about Marie's leaving. He said, "So you're on the way, Marie."

"Home, Tim. Home again. I never want to see Tony again, but that doesn't mean I don't wish him well."

"Forgive and forget, if you can. That's the thing. Remember me to your folks. I'm hoping to be back there in a year, more or less."

"That would be nice," she said. They shook hands in a sort of distant brother-and-sister way, as if remembering childhood days together.

"All aboard," Ike said, and she and he climbed into the car and took off.

"Mother," I said, "you haven't met my friend Tim Reagan."

Mother brought a hand from underneath her coat and held it out. Reagan, his hand ungloved, took it and looked into her face.

"I like to meet Jase's friends," Mother told him.

"I'm pleased to make your acquaintance."

"Would you like to come in?" she asked.

"Thanks. I can't right now."

"Excuse me, then. I'm getting cold."

Reagan, looking in her direction, made an approving nod. When she was out of earshot, he said, "I believe you now. Hell, I guess I believed you before. I'm obliged." He turned on his heel and walked away.

I went back into the house, to be greeted with a question. "What would you like for supper, Jase?"

"Anything. Quit fussing, Mother. There's more to life than pleasing menfolk. Haven't you heard of women's lib?"

"I've heard enough. I'm a liberated woman, though the likes of them wouldn't believe it. I do what I like to do."

"You ought to take a trip. Do something on your own, for yourself."

"Answer my question. What do you want for supper?"

"Plovers' eggs and smoked sturgeon. Something simple like that."

"I was thinking of stuffed pork chops."

"Fine."

It was no use to argue. She was set in her ways, and I suspected she had a point, doing what she liked to do. Yet I felt a little sad and a little guilty. Hers must be a pretty dreary existence.

I went to the phone in the living room and called Anita's number. On the first ring it struck me that Grandpa might answer the phone, and what would I say to him? Internal Revenue Service calling? County agent? Weather warning?

But Anita's voice answered, and I asked about the new man. "Just answer questions if someone's within hearing," I told her.

"It's all right. They're eating dinner." The noon meal was dinner on ranches. "Omar's all right, Jase. And he and Grandfather get along fine. I'm grateful to you."

"Don't be. I'm just glad. And one night soon I'm going to ask for time off and come to see you, if that's all right. I'll call you beforehand."

"Don't do that. Just come along."

I ate lunch and loafed around for a while, petting the dog, talking to Mother and reading. In midafternoon I bundled up and headed for the office.

I had to wait for Charleston. After a quarter of an hour he came in, took off his wraps and said, "You're earlier than need be, Jase, but all right. We'll get this business over with. Bring in Coletti, will you?"

I took the keys and went to his cell and brought him back, neither of us saying much.

"Sit down, Coletti," Charleston said from his desk.

Coletti had cured up pretty well, his bruises hardly showing. But he never would look as he had, even if he replaced the missing two teeth. He asked, "What's up now?"

"We've held you without charge, Coletti," Charleston said.

"Too damn long. Should have got me a lawyer. He'd of sprung me."

"We've held you without charge pending your wife's recovery or death."

"Yeah."

The word wasn't a question, nor could I see any interest or

concern in Coletti's dark eyes, though he must have been curious at least. All I saw was smolder.

"Now we're letting you go."

"So the bitch got well?"

"Well enough."

"I knew goddamn well she would. I just slapped her around a little."

"We saw what you'd done." The marks of dislike showed strong in Charleston's face. "I wanted her to stay and press charges against you."

"She's gone? That what you're telling me?"

"Flown the coop, as we country bums would say."

"Where?"

"Where you can't reach her and we don't want to try. That's why we're letting you out. No complaining witness."

Coletti had a quick mind, too quick. "Four stinkin' walls," he said. "Lousy chow." He was wrong there. Doolittle or Frazier or I had brought him the Commercial Cafe's best every day. "All that, and you kept me in a cage too damn long and no good reason for it."

He almost grinned, showing where his two lost teeth had been. "And that son of a bitch" — he pointed to me — "kicks my face in. Man, oh, man. Now you got no case. I know some law. I'll sue you for false arrest. I'll burn your ass."

Charleston nodded toward me, and now I thought I caught the drift. I knew why he had wanted me on hand.

"Look here, Mr. Sheriff," I said, "what's the idea, counting me out? I have a grievance. I have charges to bring. What about assault and battery? What about resisting an officer? What about attempted homicide? Throw Coletti back in a cell. Believe me, I want to be a complaining witness."

Charleston had watched Coletti while I spoke. It was his turn to grin. "I'm not forgetting about you, Jase. Your case is ironclad for a fact. But don't you think it would be best to hold back for a while?"

"What for?"

"Pending developments. Pending the suit Coletti wants to file. Hold your fire. That's my suggestion."

Coletti's voice was hardly more than a squeak. "You got me by the balls."

"It looks that way," Charleston told him. "Now get out."

"Get out of town, huh?"

"No. I wouldn't visit scum like you on an unoffending community. We don't banish bad actors. We watch them. Just get a little on the wrong side of the law, and back in jail you go. I have an idea you better beware of Tim Reagan, too." Charleston reached in a drawer and brought out an envelope. "Here's what you came with, barring a bellyful of whiskey." His thumb moved toward the rack on which we hung our wraps. "Your coat and stuff is on that peg. There's the door. Get!"

Coletti went out, giving us one baleful but defeated glance.

Charleston took a deep breath, as if the air had cleared with his going. "Nice acting, Jase. You picked up the ball fast. Now go on home, eat supper and come back later. Make it a short shift tonight if you can."

The shift not only was short: it was dull. Hardly a call came in except for routine reports. Sooner than I could imagine, I was to wish for dull times again.

I walked toward home before midnight, stopping only for a moment at the Bar Star, where Studebaker told me two carloads of hunters had gone out after wolves.

Before I reached home I heard the wild voices again, sounding hoarse and hungry in the dark well of the night. In passing, I saw that Mr. Willsie's window had been boarded up. I noticed, without much interest, that a good many porch and inside lights still burned, though the hour was late for working people. My thoughts were of Anita.

The lights at home were on, too, and Mother was still up. I greeted her and said, "Long past bedtime."

"Did you hear the wolves? Listen."

"Howling doesn't hurt anybody."

"Don't you realize that people are frightened, mothers especially?"

"They're overdoing it."

"They're escorting their children to school and meeting them when classes are over. Think of that. Being scared that wolves will make off with a little one. I've had several calls today, and what can I tell them?"

"To keep cool, I guess."

"It won't do any good to say that."

"Tell them the sheriff's office is aware, that we're looking into things, that we're prepared to take action."

"All right," Mother said, "but that won't comfort them much."

No, I thought on the edge of sleep. No sure comfort there for anxious mothers. But the alarm had no basis, no sound one. Wolves didn't prey on humans. I kept telling myself that. I went to sleep with the voices of wolves. Not sound asleep, though. I kept hearing the cries, real or imagined. The badge of office didn't guarantee peace of mind.

❖❖❖ 15 ❖❖❖

DAWN WAS JUST CREEPING INTO THE SKY when the telephone rang. My watch said seven-thirty. I grabbed the phone,
hoping it hadn't disturbed Mother. Tim Reagan was on the
line.

"Jase," he said, "damn early, I know, but could you and me
talk?"

"Now? Is it something important?"

"To me it is."

"I'll throw on some clothes and meet you at the office."

"Well." There was uncertainty in his voice.

"Why not?"

"Could be I'm making something of nothing much. And I
don't like to be laughed at."

"I won't laugh."

"I know. That's why I called you. But what about the
others?"

"Meaning the sheriff?"

"Yeah."

"Tim, he won't belittle you. I know he won't."

"I was hoping for just you and me, for now, anyhow."

"He'll have to know in time, if it's anything at all. And he's your friend, too. Believe me."

"I guess all right."

"See you in twenty minutes," I told him.

I rang Charleston then. He said he'd be on hand.

I hustled into yesterday's clothes and slipped out of the house, thankful that Mother wasn't stirring.

Tim and I arrived at the office a little ahead of Charleston. Mrs. Vail returned our greetings but didn't ask questions. She didn't have time to. The phone kept ringing. To each caller she was replying, "The sheriff's office understands and sympathizes. The whole staff is on the alert. So, we are informed, are the city police. Mr. Charleston thinks the danger is not as great as imagined, and he is advising people to keep calm. To make sure the children are safe, he has told Deputy Tad Frazier to tour the streets, morning and afternoon, when classes are about to begin and when school lets out. Please call us again if you have real reason to."

That was quite a message, but apparently it didn't satisfy one caller, for Mrs. Vail added, "No indeed, he is not minimizing the danger or trying to gloss over it. Yes. We will investigate every report."

There was a brief interval between calls, and she said, "My God, Jase! My God! They never quit ringing." Her face showed a flicker of uncertainty. "To tell the truth, I'm half-scared myself."

The sheriff's arrival saved me an answer.

We took off our coats in the inner office and sat down. Reagan looked drawn and uneasy, for want of sleep and fear of ridicule, I supposed.

Charleston asked, "Well, Tim? Something we can do for you?" He wore his easy smile.

"I don't know about that."

"It's worth a try."

I interrupted with, "We're here to listen, Tim, not to make fun of whatever it is."

Charleston nodded to my words, and we waited.

Then Reagan said, "My boys are getting the wind up."

Again we waited.

"You see, I'm kind of in charge. I'm paid a little extra to keep the gang together, and I don't know if I can."

"How so?" Charleston asked.

"There was that shooting at the Chicken Shack and Pudge Eaton dead. That's just one thing."

We could hear the buzz and the voice at the switchboard. "Jingle bells," Charleston said shortly and added, "And the other thing? Wolves, I suppose."

Reagan ignored the question to follow his own line of thought. "That brick that got throwed through some office window. We get the blame for that, but I've had my eyes and ears open, and I don't believe for a minute that one of us did it."

Charleston said, "I have my own doubts. Go on."

"This goddamn cold never gives up. We're housebound pretty much, except for the Chicken Shack. You got no idea how much propane we're burning or how much electric juice."

Charleston's head moved in agreement. "I can guess. And they call this a cold snap! What else is on your mind?"

"Then there's the town itself. Jesus, Sheriff, we ain't lepers, but that's how we're treated, not by everyone but enough. The only friendly ones are those we buy from, and that's a shitty reason."

I said, "It sure is."

"We came here to work. We was promised jobs almost right away. And here we are, bunched up and alone, and nothing to do but think about paychecks we haven't got and going broke all the time or almost. It's hard on family life. Sometimes I think I can understand that wop, Coletti. That's not exactly true. I beat him up last night."

Charleston leaned forward. "Is that what you came to tell us?"

"Naw. That's nothing. He got to bad-mouthing Marie, who I've knowed since she was a little girl. I gave him a belt for you, too, Jase."

"I'm sure he deserved it," Charleston said. "Now where were we?"

Reagan answered, "I was working around to wolves, howling every night, seems like, after we turn off the TV. I don't know wolves. I never seen one. But I've read some Jack London and so know something. Us men figure we can take care of ourselves, but the women, they don't want to be left alone. The kids, I mean the danger to 'em, worries the hell out of 'em. It's what you would call tough titty."

Reagan paused, studying our faces as if to find understanding there.

"But that's not all, is it, Tim," Charleston asked. "What more's eating on you?"

"I've already told you how we feel. Outcasts. That's what we are. And we're just simple workin' people, here to do a job. The rights and wrongs of mining ain't ours to say."

Charleston said, "No. I understand. I'm against strip mining myself, but this office is here to protect all citizens, to see to their rights. There we're on your side. You realize that?"

"Yes, sir."

"Maybe you can tell us now what really brought you here?"

"That's where you might laugh, but here goes, laugh or no laugh. It was last night, 'way late, and there was barking and howling and snapping and fighting in back of the trailers. Wolves was there, a lot of them, twenty at least. I know. I looked out, best I could, and them that weren't fighting just sat around, their tongues out. I opened the door for a better look."

I put the next question. "Can you tell a wolf from an Alsatian?"

"How's that?"

"From what is called a German police dog. There's some of them around. They can be taken for wolves."

"I don't know, but these were wolves, along with some dogs, too. And there we were, and not a damn firearm along the whole row. I went outside once, and that was enough. Don't think I scare easy, either."

He studied us, maybe suspecting amusement, then went on. "I had a ball bat, and I took it with me, and Jesus! There was a brute there that stood better than ass-high to a basketball player. He made for me, and with one bite with them jaws, he could have snapped off my leg. I ducked inside and slammed the door in his face. You believe me?"

I said, "I believe you."

"Now, more'n ever, my boys want to pack up and get out."

"Did you hear anything, see anything, before you went to bed?" Charleston asked him.

"You don't hear anything with the TV blasting away. Everybody's got a set. Everybody listens."

"Yes," Charleston said and made a face. I had heard him say once that TV was the worst drug ever visited on the American people.

"Did we see anything?" Reagan went on. "You don't get much of a rear view from a camper or trailer, not with any of them. And what can you make out if you look from a lighted room into the dark? Not much, even if you turn off the light."

"Tim," Charleston asked him, "has anyone on the row got a bitch dog? It might have come in heat."

"The only she dog I know of belongs to Clancy, and she's been what you call spaded."

Charleston rose from his chair, saying, "Let's have a look."

We put our heavy clothes back on, went out and got into one of the officer's cars. The sun showed its frosty face now. I knew better than to expect any heat from it. Bright morning, skies clear, sun shining, and no heat in the world.

We took the trail in back of the string of temporary settlement. It wasn't so much a trail as a winding of frozen ruts, churned in better weather by delivery trucks. We stopped in the rear of Reagan's mobile home. There were four or five town dogs close around, sniffing and cocking their legs at tires and steps and spare bushes. It was no use to look for paw prints, not on that stone-hard ground, or for tire marks, either, though Charleston did.

Rising, he said, "There's a bitch in heat around here. I would bet on that."

Reagan asked, "Where is she then?"

"That's the question."

Mrs. Reagan must have heard us, for she came from the trailer, buttoning up a coat. She was young but looked stooped and had an air of defeat and resentment. She asked Tim, "Any bright ideas?"

"No. Better go back in. You'll get cold."

She said, not so much to Tim as to the world, "I don't know why we stay here. What's the use? Just to spend the time keeping warm and then be scared by a bunch of wolves?"

"Now, honey."

Charleston took it upon himself to bolster her spirits. "I'm Sheriff Charleston. I wouldn't be too depressed or alarmed, Mrs. Reagan. I can guarantee that wolves won't hurt you. Remember, if you're frightened or troubled, we're within easy reach."

"Oh, sure," she answered, moving back to the door, "And while you're about it, would you mind changing the weather?"

Tim shook his head while he followed her progress. He muttered, "Can't blame her."

"We don't," Charleston told him. "Now, Tim, we can't do anything here now, but we'll learn the truth of this business. And would you make doubly sure there are no she dogs in season along the row?"

"I already know, but, sure, I'll check." He looked at the ground, as if disliking what he had to say next. "Sheriff, if it comes down to it, I wonder if you'd talk to the boys, like to me, telling them you'll stand up for their rights?"

"Whenever you say, Tim."

We left him standing there, a man puzzled and burdened by job and circumstances.

On the way to the office I asked, "Mr. Charleston, do you suppose I could have tonight off?"

He cast me a glance, grinning. "Doolittle recommends her highly."

"Ike's got good judgment but kind of a loose mouth."

His grin grew wider. "Good judgment deserves an audience." He turned back to his driving. "You'll need a car."

142

"I'm pretty sure I can borrow one."

"Nonsense." We were turning into the parking lot. "Take the car that stalled on you. Take it now. You've earned a free ride."

"Thank you. I better leave it hooked up to the juice until later."

"No need to. It's got an extra-strength battery and a new generator in it."

I said thanks again as we braked to a halt.

Charleston's parting words were, "I don't want to catch sight of you until tomorrow."

Going home, I pulled in at the Bar Star. It was a bad hour for business — ten-thirty — and Bob Studebaker was alone, wiping glasses.

"I just wanted to ask if you'd seen any wolves," I said.

"Not me. I leave that to the hunters. They charge out every night now, maybe two carloads of them, and they see plenty of wolves but can't seem to hit one. Tricky, those wolves are, just shadows and glimpses, you might say, and you can't get a good bead on a glimpse. I hear, though, that Chuck Cleaver shot one. Got the hide to prove it. But let the boys go out and waste ammunition. All right with me. Hell, they buy whiskey."

"Is your dog a wolfhound, a hunter?"

"I never asked him."

"I just wondered. You let him out at night?"

"Yeah, and last night he was mighty late getting in. Had to wake me up, barking." A quick glint came into his eyes. "Why you askin'?"

"No special reason. I thought I saw him last night."

"He ain't done anything then?"

"Nothing I know of."

Nothing, I thought as I returned to the car, nothing except scare the pants off Tim Reagan. You didn't greet a dog like Gunnar with a ball bat, not if you meant to stay healthy.

I was shaved, showered, dressed, fed and ready to go before seven o'clock that night. It puzzled me a little, on leaving the house, to see a car parked behind mine, its lights on dim. I walked toward it.

The driver's door opened, and Ike Doolittle got out, a paper bag in his hand. "This might come in handy," he said, smiling as he handed the bag to me.

"What is it?"

"What it is is a bottle. Take it along."

"That's crazy. A bottle to give to a girl!" I had a box of candy in the car.

"Grandpa likes a hot toddy." He put a friendly hand on my arm.

"I don't get it."

"You maybe will, Jase." His eyes looked up into mine, reminding me that he was a small man, a fact I kept forgetting. "Old men like him like their whiskey but don't get a hell of a lot out of it. It doesn't fire 'em up. It puts them to sleep."

"That sounds like you want me to drug him."

"A medium-size dose will do it, and it's you that will want to see that he gets it. Without a toddy he'll rattle around as long as you stay. He's not what Shakespeare would call a mewler and puker but next door to it. He's a maunderer and a cricket, mind and body, here, there and everywhere, and once in a while he'll remember to tell you to keep your mitts off his daughter. Believe me, I know."

"You seem to know a damn lot."

"Don't be touchy, Jase. No cause for it." The smile had gone from his face. "She's a prize girl, that girl, and I'm betting that custom will not stale her infinite variety. But she's a sight too young for me, Jase, and I never tried to bridge that gap, not once."

"Any more classical references?"

"Sure. 'The friends thou hast and their adoption tried . . .'" He looked up at me earnestly, and all at once I felt humble and grateful. I told him I was sorry and shook his hand.

It struck me, driving alone, that I was getting a lot of friendly help in my dating. A night off. Charleston and the car. Ike and the bottle. So what? Inside I was smiling.

The heater began to warm up the car. The night was bright with starshine. The dirt-and-gravel road smoothed out under my wheels. Away and away the land spread and rolled, frozen now but not dead, never dead. Fifteen miles to go or thereabouts. I would arrive in good time. Slow up! No need to hurry.

Once I had half-loved a waitress named Jessie Lou, a good girl who had started selling her body in the desperate hope of piling up enough money to pay for secretarial training. I had been able to help her out of that jam, and now she had a good job far away. It wasn't unpleasant to think of her. Time and distance gentled remembrance and made old affections remote. I shook hands with her, said good-bye, and drove on toward Anita.

I was a trifle surprised to come upon the Dutton house and its outbuildings so soon. I had no memory of hurrying. With the bag and the box of candy in hand I stepped to the house. There was no need to knock. Anita had reached the door before me. She cried out, "Well, Jase! Come in."

I handed her the packages, saying, "One's kind of funny, I guess."

She laid the presents on a stand table, took my things and hung them on a peg.

Grandpa and Omar were seated at the kitchen table. They looked up, and Omar said, "Hello, Mr. Beard."

"You remember Jason Beard, Grandfather," Anita said. "Jase, step closer so that he can see you better."

The old man stared at me with blank eyes. "Beard, you say? Beard?" One hand scratched at the table.

"Good evening, Mr. Dutton," I said. "I met you the other night." His eyes still were blank.

"You ought to have on your glasses, Grandfather."

"Glasses? Don't need 'em. Glasses? I can see as far as the next man."

Anita shrugged slightly, giving up. "For close vision."

"What did you say your name was?" the old man asked. "Oh, I remember. Beard. That's it. Wolf hunter, aren't you?"

"Not really. No."

Omar got up and shook my hand, as if just remembering to do so. To Grandpa he said, "He's the man got me my job with you."

"Don't you believe him. I hired you myself, didn't I?"

"Sure, Mr. Dutton, sure you did."

Anita broke in with, "Sit down, Jase, here at the table. The coffee's fresh."

She put a cup and saucer in front of me and added a plate of cookies. "Wait, though." She opened the box of candy and sought to pass it around. It came to a halt in front of Mr. Dutton. He took a piece, chewed and said, "Keep your hands off my daughter."

"Now, Mr. Dutton," Omar said.

"Please excuse him, Jase. Grandfather, forget it." There were both vexation and amusement in Anita's tone.

146

I broke up that subject by saying, "Have you seen any wolves, Mr. Dutton?"

"What you saying there?"

Before I could answer, Omar was saying, "Mr. Dutton and I come on a deer that something had killed. Looked like coyotes."

For an instant Mr. Dutton perked up. "You don't savvy wolves. It was wolves."

"Yes, sir. It was wolves," Omar answered.

"Guess what Mr. Beard brought," Anita said. "A bottle. You could have a hot toddy, Grandfather."

The old man looked around, scratching his head. "A toddy? Yeah, with whiskey. Why didn't you tell me?"

"I'll fix it. The water's hot. Omar?"

"I never touch it, Miss Anita."

"Jase?"

"With a little cold water, please."

She fixed the drinks, making herself one like mine. Grandpa reached out an eager hand. He slurped, smacked his lips and slurped again. For a little while nobody said anything much.

Then the talk turned to the weather, the feeding of livestock, the approach of calving and such absorbing subjects. The old man wasn't having any of it. His attention was on his drink. After a while, not speaking, he held out his glass to Anita. She filled it again, using no more than a dribble of whiskey.

It and what he had had were enough. He slumped by degrees. He yawned. His eyes became slow and unseeing.

Watching him, Omar pushed back from the table. "Full day tomorrow, Mr. Dutton. Bedtime for workingmen. Come on, old pardner."

The old man let himself be led away. We could hear him

fumbling around, getting ready for bed. Omar's footsteps sounded in the back of the house and quit sounding. Anita replenished our drinks.

"He's a jewel, Omar is," she said. "I'm ever so grateful to you."

"You don't need to be."

"He does what I ask him and does it well enough. And with Grandfather? Well, you noticed. And also he takes him with him when he feeds the cattle. He finds little chores for him to do. He makes him happy."

"I'm grateful to you, too," I said.

"For what?"

"For the toddy. I didn't even have to suggest it."

"I'll bet Ike Doolittle gave you the word." She smiled, showing the good white of her teeth. "He gave it to me first. Grandfather used to wander around so. He'd wake me up in the middle of the night, thinking it was breakfast time. He just couldn't sleep. Then came Ike to the rescue. What whiskey I put in the toddy can't hurt him. I checked. I think it helps him. When I forget it, Omar reminds me. That's Omar for you."

I said, "He's gentle all right. Maybe that's nature's apology for shorting his mind."

"I'm about to think that dull and gentle people have an understanding, a sort of affinity for old age and perhaps childhood, too. Or is Omar just an exception?"

"We are not ready to announce final conclusions. While our experiments tend to support what you say, they are limited and hence inconclusive."

She smiled again. "Yes, sir, professor. May I ask what your specialty is?"

"Pretty girls."

"That's nice, even if your judgment is shaky. Do you think

148

we could stand one more?" I said sure. After she had returned with the glasses, she asked, "What really are you studying in college, Jase?"

"Criminology. Aspects of the criminal mind. Psychology. Penology. Police procedures. Sociology. You name it."

"All so you can be a better policeman?"

"So I can be a better officer."

"And that's it?"

"I hope to go on. Some special branch of work. Maybe administration. Maybe advanced psychology. Maybe improved procedures. Maybe methods of investigation and investigation itself. Who can say? Meantime I have a good preceptor in Sheriff Charleston."

She took a sip of her drink. "But police work seems so limited."

"Oh, does it? Oh, sure. The public safety means nothing. Neither does the general welfare. Neither does the protection that a good officer tries to insure. Where in hell would you be without him?"

"I didn't mean to anger you, Jase." She put a hand over mine. "I was just inquiring, and I'm sorry. Please forgive me and drink your drink."

I wasn't to be put off. I knew an edge was in my voice. "People feel a good deal the same way about farmers and ranchers. It's a dumb occupation, not fit for a smart and ambitious man. Those people forget that without agriculture there would be no food on the table. Just as a good police officer has a special concern for society, so does a good farmer have a special concern for the land. We fight weeds, both of us. Wendell Berry said that a farmer was really a mother. Same thing goes in a different way for the police officer. But who cares about mothers?"

We had risen from the table. She said, "Please, Jase. Double please. I'm so sorry." She came into my arms, and anger drained out of me. I kissed her.

I said, "I got carried away. Now you forgive me."

"Nothing to forgive. You talked sense."

We kissed again. My hand felt the hard muscles of her back. They were trembling. Then rigidity went from her, and she melted against me. I felt for her breast. She moved it aside and then moved back, as if that were right.

I found myself urging her toward the front of the room, to the couch. She said against my throat, "No, Jase, please. We hardly know each other."

"I've known you forever." I wasn't quite lying. She had inhabited a thousand dreams. "It's just that we've only just met."

She drew her mouth away from mine to speak. "But Jase, when I do it, I do it for keeps. I'm not ready for keeps. I can't be. Not yet."

She tilted her head back. Her face looked swollen and infinitely sad. Her eyes, half-closed, held a glaze. It was a piteous and lovely face, the loveliest I ever had seen.

I had heard it said, in coarser language, that tumescence knew no conscience. Perhaps it wasn't conscience that deterred me. I only knew that I wanted everything between us to be clean, right and above board. Call that conscience if you will.

"I can't be ready for keeps, either," I said and released her. "I just wish I were."

"I know. I know."

I kissed her lightly and took my leave, breathing deep as I walked to the car. There was no sound of wolves on this night.

❖❖❖ 16 ❖❖❖

I WAS ON THE LATE SHIFT — was I? — on the late shift at nine-thirty, the next morning, looking at the carcass of a cow. Correction: it might have been a steer. At first blush it was hard to tell what with all the works, the genital and excretory organs, cut off or chewed off. It lay on its side in back of the trailers where we had seen the dogs sniffing.

Sheriff Charleston was there, and Ike Doolittle and probably all the residents of the row, men, women and children. They made a shivering circle around us.

Charleston was stooping, examining the cut hide. He moved up and studied the throat.

Tim Reagan asked, "What do you make of it?"

Charleston didn't answer then. "Let's turn it over," he said.

We managed that, Reagan and Doolittle and I. The carcass didn't look any better that way, but it did look different. Along the ribs the skin had been gnawed off or clawed off or cut off.

After a little more study Charleston announced, "It doesn't look like the work of wolves."

"You sure?" Reagan asked, not in dispute.

"There haven't been any cattle close around here. Seen any?"

"No, sir."

"Wolves wouldn't and couldn't have dragged the carcass here. And the kill wasn't done here."

"Chief Bandy thought different."

"He's been on hand, then?"

"A couple of hours ago," Reagan said. "His man found the carcass, touring around, and got Bandy out of bed. Bandy took a look, said wolves probably, and left to telephone I don't know who."

Charleston asked the circle of watchers, "Can any of you tell us anything? Can you help us? Unusual sounds, for instance? Perhaps something you saw?"

A shrill woman spoke up, pushing out from the circle. "You say it ain't wolves, but how in hell do you know, Mr. Wise Guy? Was you here? Did you see 'em when they sure-to-God were around? Or had you gone bye-bye? What we want is protection, not that slick salve of yours. It don't protect us. It don't protect the kids. Damn you, anyway."

Reagan managed to hush her.

Charleston said shortly, "If you remember something, tell us. This animal will be removed later. Ike, stay around. Guard the evidence. Come on, Jase." He turned to Reagan. "I have a call to make, too."

Reagan moved closer. "Could you talk to my boys later, telling them what you've told me? They're damn uneasy."

"Get them together at the Chicken Shack. Say one o'clock. I'll be there." He walked to the car, and I followed.

A man was seated in the office, waiting. Seeing him, Charleston said, "Well, Pete," and stepped ahead to shake his hand. Then he introduced me. The man was Pete Howard, a former sheriff, who had been appointed to investigate the killing and mutilation of animals, mostly cattle.

We all took seats. The muted ringing of the telephone sounded there, the almost constant ringing, and then the tones of Mrs. Vail, sounding the standard reassurance about wolves. "I was just going to call you," Charleston said to Howard.

"Bandy beat you to it."

"You've seen him and seen the carcass, then?"

"Just got here. Wanted to talk to you first. That Bandy!" His face showed contempt.

"You know him?"

"Of old. Better than I want to."

I tried to size up Howard. He was a short and stocky man with live eyes and an open face. I would have bet he was honest and competent. "You've been on the scene?" he asked.

"Yes. A man named Reagan called me."

"What's your idea, Chick?"

"I doubt this case is connected with the ones you've been investigating."

"Why's that?"

"You ever had an animal left right in town?"

"Nope. They were stumbled on, mostly in out-of-the-way places. But I suppose there has to be a first time."

"Were they branded stuff?"

"Sure."

"You'll find no brand on this one. It's been removed."

"Rib brand?"

"Like most of them these days."

"That's not predator work then. Not coyote or wolf or anything I can name. They'd go for the better and easier meat."

"It was meant to look like a wolf kill."

"Then, see here." Howard leaned forward in his chair. "If it was a man or men, why doesn't it fit into the pattern?"

I was paying attention, but another part of my mind was far off. It was with Anita and last night. I could have a job with Charleston as long as he chose to stay in office. The pay wasn't bad. It was enough. Enough for keeps. Did I want to go for keeps? One answer was yes. For the time being, at least, I could forget education. I saw that good face of hers and felt the shiver of her back under my hand, and another answer was no. No, when I used reason. No, when Grandpa came on the scene. No?

"My hunch is it doesn't," Charleston was answering Howard. "A hunch backed by some evidence. Where the carcass was, for instance. The removal of the brand. And there were no punctures in the throat of this animal."

"That's not always the mark of these butchers. Blood?"

"Very little if any. That seems to fit your pattern. Not so well, though, if the cow was killed elsewhere and hauled to town. How long would blood flow, even seep, in below-zero weather?"

"That's a thought," Howard said, relaxing. "You probably know this, but it's a funny thing, the absence of blood in the cases I know. None, you might say. None in the body cavities. We've experimented. We've tried to draw all the blood out of test animals. No luck. We've tranquilized and anaesthetized them and put pumps on the blood streams. But when one third of the blood had been drawn, the veins collapsed."

Curiosity prompted me to butt in. "Have you tried the other kind? A push pump or force pump, I mean, not the suction type?"

Howard didn't mind my intrusion. He turned to me and answered, "Yes, and we've had even less success there."

He faced back to Charleston. "Veterinarians, pathologists, toxicologists, inspectors, they've all worked with us and come up with nothing. Hell, we can't even duplicate the cut marks on the hides. Some have looked like serrations, so we've tried knives, pinking shears, even cookie cutters. No soap. A few of the cases, not the ones I've been talking about, were dismissed. Pretty obviously coyotes and birds had been at work on animals already dead."

He half-rose, as if to get up and go, but Charleston told him, "The evidence will keep. I have a man watching it."

"There's a drug called Ketaset," Howard said, settling back. "It does more than knock animals out. It increases their heartbeat almost to the breaking point. We thought we might have something there. We didn't."

"Haven't the killings and mutilations occurred in late summer?" Charleston asked.

"Most of them, and I suppose that's a point in your favor."

"This county's been lucky," Charleston said. "Not a single case, unless we have one now."

"Lucky is right. You're on the fringe of a five-county area where the Montana killings have taken place. But Montana isn't alone. Minnesota, the Dakotas, Colorado — they and others have had the same trouble. Same results, too. Zero results. But the killers seem to have gone south now. Your case, if it is one, is the first in some time."

Charleston said, "I don't believe this business of no tracks around the kills."

Howard let that one pass with a shrug. "We have more theories than we've got cases. Good God, the theories people dream up. Secret factories buying organs and blood. Blood drinkers. Wild experimenters. Devil worshipers. Witches. Followers of Isis, whoever that is. Religious cults. Prelude to the

Second Coming. The end of the world. Humans the next victims. Take your choice."

"Any hold water?"

"It's half bull but which half? We investigate them all and come out empty. We get reports, or theories, even wilder. People have seen, they say, men hooded all in black. Yep, and noiseless helicopters that leave no landing tracks. UFOs. Great hairy men, like Bigfoot. We even have a cast of his footprint. But, hell, you know most of this. Thanks for listening to me jaw away. I understand you have your own troubles?"

"One killing, unsolved."

"And wolves on top of that."

"Yeah. Wolves."

"No problem?"

"The fear is real enough."

"But not the danger, huh?"

"It's an old fear, primordial, I guess, a vestige of the times when a man had only a club to use against a saber-toothed tiger. Something like that. But danger? Hell, Pete. People have read scary stories about the far north or the steppes of Russia, but did you ever know wolves to attack human beings?"

Howard laughed and said, "Not lately," meaning never. He got up, adding, "I doubt we'll ever find the facts on this dead-cow business, but we keep trying. Out in back I have a truck with a winch on it. I want to take your animal to the lab. May need some help loading."

"Lunch first?" Charleston asked.

"Thanks, no. Two meals a day, that's my new diet."

"Deputy Ike Doolittle is watching the carcass. He'll help you load. Know where to go?"

"I think so."

Charleston gave him explicit directions.

When he had gone, Charleston said, "Time for a bite, Jase. Then to the Chicken Shack."

I wished he were sending me to the Dutton ranch and Anita. Half of me was there.

We had hamburgers at the Commercial Cafe and spent some time over coffee. About all that was said was said by Charleston. "If anyone gets to the bottom of this business, it'll be Pete Howard. Good man. Thank the Lord it's his baby, not ours."

A dozen or so men had gathered at the Chicken Shack. Some I didn't know. Some I knew by sight. Then there were Tim Reagan and Tony Coletti. All looked like workingmen, not ranch-type workingmen, but like machinists and operators of heavy equipment. Some wore their hard hats.

Ves Eaton was tending bar or, rather, leaning on it, for he had no customers. I imagined Reagan had cautioned the bunch about drinking.

We got rid of our coats and caps, and Reagan introduced Charleston, saying only, "This here's Sheriff Charleston. I asked him to talk to us."

Charleston stood up while he spoke. He took a long minute to look around first, sizing up the crowd. They were attentive enough.

"I'm not here to give a pep talk to you men," he began. "Let's face the facts. An element in this county, a substantial element — I'm speaking of people — hates to think about farm land torn up, about range land ripped open by strip mining. They oppose you, of course. My own sentiments are no matter. The duty of my office is to see that the laws are obeyed. Neither, as Mr. Reagan has said, are the rights and wrongs of strip mining your proper concern. You came here to work, came at the bidding of the company that employs you. In that sense you are innocent. You might, though, think of your opponents not as enemies but people of a different turn of mind."

While he paused a man I didn't know asked a question. He was a wiry-looking, red-headed man, and he called out, "How about Pudge Eaton?"

"I'm coming to that," Charleston answered, unruffled. "Most of the people who fight against strip mining are decent people. They will stand against you as long as they can, but they will accept what the environmental agencies say. If it comes to court, they will abide by what the court decides. I know that, and you must believe it."

"We don't have to believe nothin'," the redhead put in.

Charleston just looked at him and went on. "I said most of the people. I didn't say all. It's plain that some men, maybe only one man, have a scheme to scare you out of the country, away from your jobs. You can call it a conspiracy, a nonviolent conspiracy."

A man I didn't know broke in. "Pudge Eaton gets killed, and it's not violent. Bullshit."

"It wasn't meant to be violent. The man with the rifle was shooting out lights. He made a bad shot. The bullet hit one of the porch supports and veered up. Eaton wasn't a target. We have proof of that."

The unknown man let out, "Ha!"

"That was the start of the campaign," Charleston continued. "Next we have dogs, or possibly wolves, the bunch that came together in back of your places. Finally, there's the dead cow this morning in about the same place. It was meant to look like the work of wolves. It wasn't."

The red-headed man was persistent. He said, "Them wolf howls at night. What about them?"

"I don't know. I intend to find out."

158

"Somebody's got a pet wolf pack." That was Coletti, sneering as he spoke.

Reagan said, "Shut up, Coletti. Shut your damn mouth."

The miner I didn't know interrupted again. "It's all guesses. You haven't come up with a goddamn thing, not a real thing. You can't salve us with bullshit."

"I'm telling you what I'm sure of." Charleston remained unperturbed. "Bits and pieces are coming together. I begin to see the end."

As he paused, Reagan said, "Thank you, Mr. Charleston," as if the meeting was over.

It wasn't. Charleston had a last word. "I've let you in on what I know, but there's one other thing. My office will protect your rights. The yes and no of strip mining are not your concern, but the rights of American citizens are our concern as much as they are yours. We will honor and protect those rights. Should anyone do you wrong, let us know. You'll get action."

Reagan thanked him again. There was some applause. Charleston and I took our leave.

Howard and the carcass were gone from the alley, and so would be Doolittle. Driving on, Charleston said, "Tomorrow we're going to talk more to Chuck Cleaver."

We weren't though, because by that time Chuck Cleaver was dead.

❖❖❖ 17 ❖❖❖

IT WAS ELEVEN-THIRTY that same night, and I was about to knock off. I had had time to nap, eat, look over the reports from the switchboard and type an account of the day's events. Then the telephone rang.

"Jase," Ike Doolittle said into my ear, "I just got a report of a man shot dead."

"Who?"

"Don't know."

"Where?"

"Out there where they been huntin' wolves. That's all was told me."

"Who called?"

"Search me. Wouldn't give a name. Man's voice."

"Why call you, not the office?"

"Search me again."

"You are home?"

"Yeah. In my room."

"We won't call Mr. Charleston yet. It may be some joker. You dressed?"

"Take me a minute."

"I'll go warm up a car and wait for you."

Blanche Burton was about to knock off, too. I told her, "Leave a note for Mrs. Carson. We might need the sheriff tonight, but she's not to call him unless we say to."

"What's up, Jase?" she asked me.

"Maybe nothing. Maybe another killing."

"Who? What in the world —?"

I left her wondering.

Doolittle showed up soon after I had started the car and got the heater blowing. "You know those roads better than I do," I said, "so how about driving?" I moved over to the passenger side.

For a while we were too busy rubbing and scraping our frosted breath from the windshield to do much talking. After a while I said, "This is damn funny business. Did you recognize the man's voice?"

"Who can put a name to a voice over a scratchy line?"

"And no clue as to where to go?"

"Just the whole damn scoop of country. Somewhere where the wolf hunters rolled."

We drove on, silent. I was hoping the call was a false alarm, and probably Doolittle was, too. The bleak country flowed around us, dark and still. A faint starlight showed on level and ridge. We had to hold up to let four gaunt deer cross the road. It was hard going for wild creatures, I thought, and not too dandy for tame. It was no country to live in, and it was mine. Come spring, I would laugh at past discomforts, counting them nothing. I asked if the heater was on full tilt. We passed the Linderman place and, later, the Whitney buildings. Both were dark, as they wouldn't be, we agreed, if the occupants had heard of a killing.

"Those wolf hunters could have taken off nearly anywhere,"

Doolittle said. "Didn't have to follow the roads. Not many fences to stop them and no snow. They could have cross-hatched the whole damn country." We kept on, watching to see what our light revealed and straining to see beyond their shine.

It was a long search, apparently futile, and then, a hundred yards off the road, a pickup truck loomed. Doolittle steered toward it. A shape lay at its tailgate.

We got out, taking flashlights, and stepped ahead. A north wind, colder than death, began playing with us. The shape lay spraddled, face down. We turned it over. The flashes showed the bloody, torn face of Chuck Cleaver.

"Good God!" Doolittle said, drawing back. "The poor bastard!"

"Shot in the back of the head."

"Uh-huh."

"I bet by wolf hunters," I said. "He was hunting himself." I pointed to a rifle that had fallen from Cleaver's grip. "Must have been a hunter who called you." I took hold of Cleaver's hand and tried to move his arm. Death had already stiffened him, death or the cold.

"Get on the radio, Ike," I said. "Get word to Charleston. He'll rout out the others. You can tell where we are better than I can."

Doolittle hurried to the car, leaving me for a minute with death and that deathly wind. Charleston had been right. Those hearty wolf hunters with whiskey in their bellies were bound to do somebody in. I felt more and more certain that one of them had called in the report, refusing to give his name because he or one of his party was guilty.

Doolittle came from the car, saying, "Message sent."

I asked him, "Just where are we? Do you know?"

He didn't answer at once. He squinted north, south, east and west. "Yeah, I know."

"Tell me then."

"The Dutton place is over that hump, mile or so away. Can't see it from here, or any lights."

"You sure Mrs. Carson got the message right?"

"Yep. Sheriff was going to tail up Doc Yak and Underwood."

"While we wait, I have plenty of time to go tell Anita."

"I don't know, Jase. I got a feeling we ought to stay here."

"You can stay. I won't be gone but a few minutes."

"Long enough for me to freeze solid."

"You can get in the truck, away from the wind."

"I hate to think of you waking up the household, including old Grandpa."

"I'll be mighty quiet. You'll be warm enough. Start up the truck and turn on the heater."

"Not me. I'm not going to fiddle with it. Not me, messing up evidence."

"I just want —"

"I know what you want, Jase. All right, then." He started walking to the truck. I guessed, with some astonishment, that he didn't like to be alone in the presence of death.

I wheeled our car back to the road and set out. Once over the hump I could see the Dutton house. The lights were on.

The radio crackled. Mrs. Carson asked, "Ike?"

"No. Jase."

"Jase, Sheriff Charleston and the rest are on the way."

I thanked her and drove on.

I coasted the car to the front of the house and took care not to slam the door when I got out. I stepped to the house and knocked softly.

Anita came at once, a finger to her lips.

I said, "Anita, I came to tell you —"

She made a hushing sound. "Don't come in. You'll disturb him. Grandfather's very sick. I think it's pneumonia."

"You called a doctor?"

"That new man in Petroleum. He said he'd come just as soon as he could. He told me what to do."

"Doc Yak's coming this way. You want him?"

"No need." An instant later she asked, "What's bringing Doc Yak?"

"That's what I came to tell you. Chuck Cleaver's been shot, out wolf hunting."

"Chuck Cleaver? Dead?"

"Yes."

"Dear Lord!" she said. "Chuck Cleaver."

A strangled, frail cry came from inside the house.

"That's Grandfather. I've got to go. Good-bye, Jase." She gave me time for the quickest of kisses.

I drove back to Cleaver's truck. Doolittle came from it, slapping himself against the cold. "Quick trip," he said.

"Too quick. Grandpa's down with maybe pneumonia. Mrs. Carson said help's on the way."

We waited, for safety's sake running the engine and heater just now and then. Presently we saw headlights coming our way. They belonged to an ambulance and Charleston's old Special. We directed the three men to Cleaver's body. Doc Yak bent over it, his doctor's bag in one hand.

"Dead," he said almost at once. "Stone dead, as you might say. I wish to Christ, Charleston, that sometime you'd take me to someone I could help."

"Me, too," Charleston answered, "but we have to have a doctor's certificate."

"Goddamn red tape. Without a certificate I suppose the poor son of a bitch would be alive. But all right. Bullet wound.

Looks bigger than a .22, probably not as powerful as a .30-06. That's at first blush."

"No idea about time of death, Doc?"

"Oh, sure." Doc's breath made abrupt clouds of white. "Not hard, not with this warm zephyr blowing. Make it he was killed sometime, as he sure as hell was."

Felix Underwood said, "Well?"

"Take him away, Felix. Take him where it's nice and warm. Take me, too. That damn Charleston believes in cruel and inhuman treatment."

Doc fastened the case he hadn't used. Felix took a stretcher out of the ambulance, and Doolittle and I helped him lift the body to it and carry it on to the ambulance.

Charleston poked around with a flashlight and shook his head. He picked up the rifle with a gloved hand. With only the three of us left, he said, "Keys in the truck?"

Doolittle told him they were.

"Sorriest chore of all," he said, pausing for a moment. "Telling people about sudden death. Jase, bring the truck to the Cleaver ranch. Just follow me. Ike, take the other car to town."

The truck started easy enough, and I lumbered the five or six miles to the Cleaver place, watching Charleston's headlights bobbing ahead of me.

The house was dark, huddled against the cold, hibernating, I thought, as if sleep alone were the answer to weather like ours. Charleston knocked at the back door and knocked again. Finally we heard movement inside, and Mrs. Cleaver opened the door. She had on an old wrapper around her. Her hair hung in strings. Seeing who we were, she said, "He ain't here. He's out hunting wolves."

"We came to see you, Mrs. Cleaver. May we come in?"

She stood aside, not speaking until after we'd entered. "Better come to the front room," she said. "There's maybe some heat left in the stove." There may have been some. The old livestock dog that we had seen before was lying by the stove. She got up, sniffed at us and, satisfied, went back and lay down again.

"Won't you sit down, Mrs. Cleaver?" Charleston asked. She let herself perch on a chair, hugging herself against the creeping cold. We took tentative seats on that old, worn furniture. "I'm sorry," Charleston continued. "It's bad news we bring."

"Might as well spit it out then."

"Your husband has been shot. He is dead."

Her expression hardly changed. She had the face of a cow, I thought, a face dull to tragedy, dull to death and loss. She might have been listening to the last of a series of blows that had left her shockless. "He's gone," she said, as if letting the words sound in her mind. "I told him that wolf huntin' would be the end of him. I told him to stay home. But, no. Like all them crazy hunters, he had to go out."

"I'm sorry. Jase, will you give Mrs. Cleaver the details?"

I told her about the phone call, the caller unidentified, the search for the body and where we found it. While I talked, Charleston stared at a bookcase, which might have had thirty volumes in it. From where I sat, I couldn't make out the titles. I laid the stare to Charleston's love of books.

He picked up when I left off. "Did Mr. Cleaver go hunting often?"

"Regular lately."

"Did he get any wolves?"

"A time back, he got one. Just a couple or so of coyotes since then. The skins are in the tool shed, if you want to see." She rose, a gaunt, worn woman, and put a chunk of wood in the stove. "Maybe it'll catch."

166

Here, I thought, watching her, was a marriage held together by habit, by hardship, by erosion of soul, until feeling was lost and communication made mute. It would be different with Anita and me.

She went back to her chair and spoke in a stronger yet plaintive tone. "Now what'll I do? Him gone, what'll I do?"

Charleston said, "It's hardly a time to decide, Mrs. Cleaver. Don't think about it now."

"I can't run this ranch by myself." She thrust a stringy arm from under the wrapper. "You can see that. I got to decide. Waitin' won't help."

Now a tear came to one eye and rolled down her cheek, a tear for the loss of working muscle.

Charleston took a breath and sighed it out. "How do you feel about the ranch?"

"Nothin'. I never felt nothin' much, not after the shine had wore off. Just cold and wind. Just lonesomeness. Just work. And what's to show for it? A few ornery cows and the wolves howlin'."

Charleston surprised me by saying, "Then I would lease the mineral rights, the rights to mine coal. You understand?"

"Chuck would turn over in his grave if he was in it yet." She looked up. "But he's gone now. I guess he wanted to be buried in the town cemetery, but he never quite said so. We didn't talk about passin' away or anything else much. Not lately. I got to see about buryin' him."

"We'll be glad to make the arrangements you want," Charleston told her.

"Lease it, you said?"

"Yes. That is if you need the money."

"When was it we didn't?"

Charleston went on to explain. "Right now you can get a

good price. Here's what to consider. If strip mining goes through, your land won't be worth much as a ranch. Your husband understood that. But it hasn't been approved yet and won't be for some time. Maybe never. If it isn't approved, you'd still have your ranch. Is that plain enough?"

"I don't know. I just don't know."

"Think about it. We have to be on our way. Would you like to ride to town with us? Stay with somebody tonight?"

"No. I'll set right here. If I get the wide eye, Chuck's got a bottle he thinks is hid."

"You're sure?"

" 'Course I am. I'm alone mostly anyhow."

Charleston got to his feet. "The body's on its way to the undertaker's. You can see it later if you wish."

"Don't fret yourself about me. Nobody does." Another tear came to one eye.

We said good-bye and made for the tool shed, Charleston muttering, "Home, sweet home."

He examined the four skins we found on stretchers in the tool shed and announced, "One's a wolf all right. Or looks like a wolf."

As we rode along to town, he broke a long silence. "Jesus, Jase, I'm afraid the shit is about to hit the fan now." Raw language was uncommon to him. It came from disturbance.

"You mean trouble?"

"Yes. Conflict."

"But you told me a violent death calmed things down."

"The shoe's on the other foot."

"I don't get it."

"There are more ranchers than strip miners, more on one side than on the other. Watch out when you sting majorities. Understand now?"

"I guess so," I said, and maybe I did.

❖❖❖ 18 ❖❖❖

THE WEATHER BROKE in the early morning. The wind woke
me up, though I was half dead for sleep. It sang and sighed
at the windows and the house corners, and the house itself
murmured, and I threw off some covers, thinking slowly that
a chinook had at last come. I drifted back to sleep with its
singing.

Walking to work late that afternoon, I felt buoyant, lifted
in step and spirit by the warm wind out of the west. You could
almost hear the land relaxing, freed of the tight clamp of the
cold. It was breathing again, and hope rode on the air.

And so it was with the townspeople and those who had
floated in from the country. Cars stood at the curbs, and men
and women popped in and out of doorways, rid now of their
cumbersome wraps. They stopped me, some of them did, and
spoke in the strong voices of cheer. First item, the weather
and wasn't it great? Second item, poor Chuck Cleaver killed
and what did I know about that? Mike Day, the banker, stood
outside his place in his suit coat. "Never lose faith," he told

me solemnly. "Remember the silver lining. Too bad about Cleaver. Accidental, you think?"

"All I know is no silver lining for him," I answered and walked on.

I stopped at the public telephone booth and called Anita. "He may be a little better," she said in answer to my question about her grandfather. "Yes, the doctor's been here twice. He left pills and instructions and said he'd be back."

"I wish I could see you."

"Not now, Jase. Not while I'm nursing an invalid."

She didn't think to ask about Cleaver. She had her own worries.

Charleston sat in his office, doing nothing unless thinking was something. "You're early," he said.

"I had plenty of sleep. What about you, Mr. Charleston? You look as if you could use some."

"I'll stick around for a while."

I sat down at my desk and the typewriter. As I inserted a sheet, he said, "I would wish the weather hadn't broken so soon."

"What! Everybody's enjoying it."

"I know," he said and went on thinking and presently added, "It may be nothing and probably is, but cold weather puts a crimp in people and warm weather takes the crimps out. Ask any demonstrator. Ask rioting students."

He left me to reflect on his words while I sketched out a report of last night. Finally he asked, "You want to bring me a sandwich, Jase?"

"Sure. But I'm here, so why stay on?"

He answered only, "Seems best."

So I walked to the Commercial Cafe, crowded in and managed to get a hamburger to go. I knew he would have his own coffee.

Six o'clock came, and seven and eight, and then the phone rang. He listened and said, "Right away," hung up and told me, "Come along, Jase." He took time to add, as we hurried from the office, "That was Doc Yak."

While I broke the engine-heater connection, he jumped into the car and flung a door open for me. He found a parking place close to the Bar Star. We could have walked the same distance and lost little time. From outside we could hear a racket inside the place.

Depending on the location of home, the Bar Star was called, only half-jokingly, the uptown office or the downtown office. Deals were made there. Buyers of livestock passed checks to sellers. Ranchers contracted for feed stuff. Passers-by dodged in to get warm. Committees met and laid plans. Poker players could be accommodated. Serious drinkers could forget home, if they had one, and those who didn't could find ease for their loneliness. It was at once business place, retreat and point of assembly.

We stepped in to find a crowd of men, numbering twenty or more. The place smelled of spilled beer, tobacco smoke and bodies. Doc Yak drank alone at the head of the bar. A man was holding forth. He was Jim Burke, the auto mechanic with the big family, and he was saying, "Let's go! Them earth-diggers ruin the country and kill men besides. Goddamn the likes of them, shootin' Chuck Cleaver. Put the run on 'em, that's what I say. Who's with me?"

He received shouts of support, but one by one the men fell silent as they caught sight of Charleston. The speaker turned around and saw him, too.

Charleston asked quietly, "What goes on?"

Bodie Dunn spoke now, "It's no matter to you. It's our business."

"What business is that?"

Francis Fournier, the part-blood, answered. "What's it to you if we just turn over a couple of them sheep-wagons they call home? They'll vamoose then."

"And close down that Chicken Shit place," Burke put in. "While you draw your pay, we'll do your damn work."

"And get even for Cleaver," Dunn said.

Charleston said, "I wouldn't try that." He stood there, solid, unmoving, while his hard eye went from one man to another. He should have been a general.

"Who cares?" Burke asked, his voice loud. "Bunch of goddamn foreigners!"

Charleston raised his tone. "Whatever they are, they're Americans. Free Americans, entitled to the protection of American laws."

"Throwin' bricks through windows is one thing," Bodie Dunn said, "but by God killin' one of us is another. Americans, you say? Bullshit!"

"And who's to say we can't do it?" Burke shouted. "Who's to say?"

"The sheriff of the county."

"You and your peedad crew. We elected you and we can, by God, unelect you."

"Meantime, I'm the sheriff, and the laws will be observed."

"Piss on that noise. What say, gang?" Burke moved forward two steps, and the crowd moved with him.

Charleston held up a hand. "God gave you heads. Use them. Run off the strip miners and you lose the killer, if he's among them."

Francis Fournier said, "There are ways, many ways, to make men talk. We make them talk."

"That's it. We'll have 'em squealing. What say, gang?" That was Burke again.

The men were restive, eager for action. There was energy here, wild energy, fed by a killing and release from the cold. I felt myself bracing. I could take out one of them, maybe two. Charleston could do as well or better. Tackle the leaders first. Yeah, those leaders — Burke, an indifferent mechanic; Dunn, hardly more than a handyman; Fournier, a barely successful rancher. It was in the book, the books I had studied. The prejudiced, the stupid, the vociferous led mobs and, too often, parties.

I caught movement at the other side of Charleston, and there stood Ike Doolittle with a double-barreled shotgun in his hands. Little Doc Holliday, siding with the Earp brothers at the O.K. Corral. And from the front of the bar came Bob Studebaker with Gunnar on leash.

Charleston said, "None of that, Ike. Put it in a corner."

"You men go fighting the law, and, God help me, I turn the dog loose," Studebaker announced.

The interruptions gave Charleston a break. He spoke quietly now. "Listen to me, men. We don't know who's guilty. It might be a strip miner. It's more likely to be a wolf hunter who shot Cleaver by accident. He would be trying to cover up now. He would be trying to mislead you, to make you suspect somebody else. Some of you have hunted wolves. One of you may be the guilty party. I do not say that this is so. I say it may be. The innocent, including those of you who haven't hunted, surely will want to find out. That's what I and my crew want to do."

The men began looking, one at another, with beginning

wonderment in their eyes. Doc Yak was smiling into his glass. Studebaker held Gunnar in check.

Doc Yak yelled, "Belly up to the bar, boys. On me. Generous to a fault and poor to boot, that's yours truly. Belly up."

Driving back to the office, Charleston said, "We won the ball game, but it was close." There was no victory in his voice, just strain and fatigue. "From now on keep your own hours. Put full time on the Cleaver case, Jase."

"Subject to help, I hope," I said.

"All we can give. I'll drop off at the Jackson Hotel."

I didn't see him until the next afternoon, meantime keeping busy myself.

◆◆◆ 19 ◆◆◆

THE CASE WAS MINE, and a man assigned to a case got with it, even if his task involved largely just the preliminaries, as I suspected mine did. Charleston would come on the scene, surely, after my initial appearance.

I set out at eight o'clock, my immediate destination the Jope Jordan ranch. Charleston hadn't mentioned him last night, and for a good reason. You didn't make public the name of a suspect until you had proof and, better yet, the man under arrest. But it was certain Jordan had been in his mind. Jordan had threatened Cleaver after Cleaver had knocked him down as the environmental meeting came to an end.

Jope wasn't Jordan's given name, of course. When he made the local news, which was seldom, he appeared in print as Joseph P. Jordan or Joe P. Jordan. In earlier days another Joe Jordan had lived in the county, so my father had told me. To avoid confusion, then, the man I wanted to see had been referred to as Joe P., later shortened to Jope by citizens saving of syllables.

The car purred along. The chinook wind still blew. To the west the mountains stood sharp as scissor cuts. To the east the land rolled and fell away until earth and sky embraced. North and west was my direction, toward the furred foothills. I didn't need the car heater. A warm, clean, far-seeing day.

I drove past the Cleaver place and, next to it, two miles farther on, came to Jope Jordan's ranch. I couldn't see a head of stock on it, not a cow or a horse or a sheep or even a hen. The outbuildings — the barn and tool shed and chicken house — were closed and nothing moved near them. But a plume of smoke came from the house and ran into tatters as the chinook took it. It alone gave evidence of life here.

Jordan answered my knock and said, "Hello, Beard. Come inside, won't you?" I was having my first hard look at him. He wasn't quite so tall as I. He wore suspenders over slumped shoulders. His seamed face had the marks of wind, sun and cold and, I thought, maybe the bottle. It appeared pleasant enough.

We sat near the wood heater, which radiated the little warmth that was needed. The rooms, from what I could see of them, were sparsely furnished, as if the owner were soon to take leave. The walls were marked where furniture had been.

"Something on your mind?" he asked after we were seated.

"I suppose you heard that Chuck Cleaver got killed?"

"How could I miss it? I've kept a radio and TV while selling off the rest of my stuff bit by bit. And the telephone. Sure, I've heard. We weren't friends, Cleaver and me, but I'm sorry."

"You two had a fight."

"He belted me one all right, and I said things I for sure didn't mean."

"I was there. Remember?"

He nodded. "Chuck wouldn't use his head, not that it was too sharp when he used it. His ranch isn't worth much. Neither is mine. So along came those lease hounds and offered good money and more money if you played hard to get. That's what I did. Chuck wouldn't go along."

I said, "I know."

"I got tired of ranching. It's damn tough even on good land. And then my wife up and died eight months ago, and what was I to do? Play hermit like old Linderman? Just chug along to the graveyard? Not for me. I took the money. I'll head out pretty soon."

"You weren't mad at Cleaver?"

"For a minute. That's all. When he biffed me. He claimed if my land was mined, his would be ruined, graze and water and all. Now who can tell about that? What's more, if a man owns a chunk of land, he has a right to do with it whatever he pleases. Right?"

"That's the frontier idea."

He smiled then, a friendly smile. "I'm old-fashioned, but, still, I wouldn't push that notion too far. But it came down to cases, and I voted to lease. Do you blame me? Hey, how about a drink before you answer?"

"Thanks, no. That's no reason for you not to have one."

He got up, went to an old cabinet and poured two fingers in a not very clean glass. He said, "Good bourbon," and looked at me inquiringly. I shook my head.

When he had reseated himself, glass in hand, I told him, "It's not for me to blame you for leasing. Your business, not ours. Ours is to find out who killed Chuck Cleaver."

"I sure as hell wish you luck."

"So I have to ask questions. The first one is: Where were you night before last when he was shot?"

Jordan took a swallow of his drink and smiled. "Now, son, you think you have a right to quiz me?" He was anyhow twenty years older than I, so the "son" wasn't offensive.

"It's a simple question."

"It's answers that come hard, answers to anything. Like why are you alive? Why me? Where's the real reason?"

He was playing with me, I came to realize, and that knowledge nettled me. "I'm not a philosopher," I told him. "You don't have to answer. You can demand an attorney."

He laughed then, a real laugh that rippled the whiskey in his glass. "I see you know the rules, son. Now let me see. Night before last? It kind of beats me, trying to remember." He finished his drink and smiled genially. "Were the wolves howling that night?"

"Why do you ask?"

"Might help me to remember. Were they?"

"I think so. I'm not sure."

"You see? You can't remember yourself. Can't answer for certain. We're in the same boat."

He rose and poured himself two more fingers of bourbon. He sat down and looked at me, waiting.

I said, "I still want to know where you were night before last."

"I'm coming round to it. What's wrong with a friendly talk, with tossing some bullshit around? I have damn few visitors since my wife died."

"We can visit another time."

"You're awful serious, son. But all right. All right." He downed his whiskey in a gulp, got up, went to a wardrobe, fumbled in it and came out with a slip of paper. He handed it to me. It was a receipt for three-nights' lodging at the Rest Easy motel 70 miles away from the ranch.

I read it and told him, "It still doesn't prove that you were there all the time."

"Right you are. Ever play poker?"

"Only a little."

"That's what I was doing, some old sidekicks and me, playing straight poker, jacks or better to open, when Chuck got himself shot."

"Names of those sidekicks?"

"Sure. Four of 'em. You see, I was blowing some of my ill-gotten gains, staying in the city, drinking a little, playing cards. You want names, I'll give them to you along with a couple of addresses. The rest you can look up. Got a pencil and paper?"

After I had made my notes, I said, "We'll check, but it looks like you're clear. It took a long time to get it out of you, though."

"Here I was, wantin' company, and if I had answered straight out, you would have rolled away pronto. Straight question, straight answer, so long." He laughed. "Cagey old bird, that's me. Now have a good-bye drink."

I took one with him, said my thanks and shook his hand before leaving.

Charleston had suggested I see Mrs. Cleaver, make sure she was all right and talk of funeral arrangements, so I stopped there on my way back to town. I walked by the parked truck and saw her at the entry, gazing out with the dull look of a cow watching through an open barn door. She said, "It's you again."

"We wanted to find out if you were all right. How are you getting along?"

"Good as you could expect. I just boiled some coffee. Come in if you want to."

I sat at the kitchen table. She poured coffee in mugs and took a seat opposite me. The coffee smelled scorched. It was as bitter as acid.

"Is there anything you need, Mrs. Cleaver? One of us could bring it out."

"God hisself couldn't bring all I need."

"I mean groceries, anything like that?"

"I ain't much for meat, though I got some, and plenty garden stuff that I canned."

"That's good. Now another thing. Viewing the body? I could take you into town now if it suits you?" If it did suit her, I would have to wait until she changed clothes. What she wore looked like a wool sack.

"Me see him?" she said. "Look at him dead?"

"You know Mr. Underwood. He's very good at —"

She took the finish away from me. "— at makin' 'em look alive."

"Let's say natural."

"My mind's eye sees him clear. That's enough."

"Then about the funeral?"

"Sooner the better, I say. What's the good of keepin' a body around?"

"Tomorrow, then? Say two o'clock?"

"That's good enough."

"The family usually picks out a casket?"

"You folks do it for me. Not fancy. I guess you better round up some preacher, too."

I said, "We'll attend to those things. Do you drive?"

"Nothin' to drive but that old truck. It wouldn't be fittin' for mourning. Chuck was always goin' to buy a passenger car. Never got around to it. Not enough money, though he spent it for other things."

"Mr. Underwood will send a car out for you. That's part of his service."

"Charges for it, too, I bet, but it's accommodatin'."

"That's all settled then?"

"Not some things," she said. "What you know about leases?"

"They've been here already?"

"Already twice."

I wasn't surprised. Widows, even if newly made, were easy meat for lease hounds and other keen businessmen.

I took a sip of coffee acid as Mrs. Cleaver went on. "I ain't signed. What's a fair price? I got to know that."

"Don't settle yet," I told her. "You know Judge Bolser? Fine. Talk to him. He's up on things."

"Then," she said, "I'm going to get shut of all our stuff." A sweep of her arm embraced house, outbuildings and land. "Ranch, cows, kettles, all of it."

"And live in town?"

"Live somewhere else, that's where."

I was glad to say good-bye. Poor old dame, deadened to all but self-concern. Poor Chuck Cleaver, soon to lie in the grave-yard. Poor match. Poor Linderman, too, depending on the dependence of his animals. Poor Jope Jordan, lonely for company. Poor women who worked at our switchboard, hoping for a last fling at romance that time said would turn sour. Life didn't have to frazzle into sad tags. It didn't have to grow narrow and mean. It wouldn't with me if I had my way. I wouldn't let it.

What with driving and conversation, morning and noon

time had passed. For old time's sake, sure, old times, I went to the Jackson Hotel for a late lunch and imagined Anita sitting opposite me. After eating, I called her. She wasn't encouraging either about her grandfather or a visit from me. I couldn't blame her, seeing her hovering over a sick bed.

Next on my list was Bodie Dunn. I learned at the Bar Star that he was helping unload some freight cars. He wouldn't want to be interrupted at work. Amendment: his boss wouldn't want him to be interrupted.

I drove to the Chicken Shack. What the hell else was there to do? What else to do when, for all I knew, another man was being blasted? Could I ride herd on the whole damn country? Was I supposed to have x-ray eyes? Was I Mr. Hear All, See All, Know All? The man of action, the super-sleuth, the public protector, he had a bellyache.

Ves Eaton was behind the bar. On stools in front of it were Tim Reagan and three miners I knew only by sight. The miners spoke to me civilly, perhaps having heard of last night's face-down, perhaps for other reasons, including Tim's friendly greeting. I beckoned him to a table after telling Eaton I would buy a round, small beer for me, please.

Reagan came over and sat down, a glass in his hand. "We're getting to be a bunch of goddamn drunks," he said. "No work, and what else is there to do? Watch that fool picture box until you scream bloody murder. Talk until talk plays out. Keep scratching your butt, then go to boozing."

"You handle it all right," I told him.

He smiled. "Until that one time when you taught me my manners."

"Forget it."

"Anyhow, thanks for standing up to 'em last night."

"It wasn't me. It was the sheriff and Doolittle and Studebaker with that big dog. I was just there."

"On the front line, I heard."

I shook off that subject. "I'm trying to nose out who shot Chuck Cleaver. Sheriff's orders."

"Don't forget Pudge Eaton."

"We haven't."

"Connection?"

"Maybe. Who knows?"

Reagan sipped at his drink and said mildly, "So you come to me?"

"I have to, Tim. It could have been one of your boys."

He shook his head. "I bet my shirt it wasn't."

"Still?"

"The only real bad apple in the bunch is Coletti, and he's a knife man. I swear, Jase, there's not a rifle on the row. Not a single one. Revolvers and such is different. There's some around, bought just for protection against wolves, but they're snub-nosed and mostly small caliber. It was a rifle that kilt the man, wasn't it?"

"That's how it looks. But all right, Tim. Now would you help me out? Do some of my work?"

"That's okay. What?"

"You know. Smell around. Talk. Ask questions. Tell me if you find out anything."

"All right. Sure. Dead end, though. But it gives me an interest beyond this damn drinking." He lifted his glass and looked at it. "Damn stuff."

We dawdled away a couple of hours, making small talk and drinking only a little. I looked at my watch for perhaps the tenth time and said, "I have to talk to Bodie Dunn. About quitting time for him."

"Don't believe what that son of a bitch says."

I left my chair. "I know him. Don't worry."

Bodie Dunn sat in a booth at the Bar Star, glaring at a beer. Except for Studebaker and two customers on stools, he was the only one there. I slid into the booth. "Just when I was gettin' comfortable," he said to the beer, "here comes a buttinsky, and damn his soul."

"Any further remarks?" I asked him.

His eyes lifted to me then. They were small eyes, angry yet furtive. "You got people lookin' sidewise at me, like as if I had pot-shot Chuck Cleaver."

"Did you?"

He made a violent gesture, upsetting his beer. "I ought to knock your nose back to your neck." What he dared to do was something less than what he proposed.

Studebaker arrived with a bar towel and began wiping up. "And you!" Dunn said to him. "You're as bad as the rest. Why do I come into this fuckin' bar?"

"You must like it," Studebaker said easily. I asked him to bring Dunn another beer.

After its delivery I said, "I have to ask questions."

Again Dunn's eyes lifted to me. "Ask your head off. See if I care."

"Could you, or anyone with you, have shot Cleaver by accident, thinking he was a wolf? You were shooting pretty wild, at anything that seemed to move."

"Now you got it," he said, spreading his hands. "I own up. But it was his truck we were shootin' at, takin' it for a wolf. Cleaver just happened to get in the way."

"Thanks. I'll put it down as an accident. One truck shot and killed. Bring the hide in."

"I'm laughin' fit to kill."

"Me, too, at you. Who was with you on your expeditions?"

"Different times, different guys."

"You know, Dunn, for two-bits I'd haul you in and let Charleston lean on you. He takes killing serious. You damn better do the same."

"Who doesn't?" He took a long look at his beer, the bluster seeping out of him. "Honest to God, Beard, we'd of known if we shot Cleaver. We wouldn't of buttoned up or turned tail. I swear to that. Now think on it. The truck was right there, alongside where I heard you found him. We wasn't that drunk, not to notice, and none of us shot him. If Charleston wants to use his rubber hose, that's all I can tell him."

"No rubber hose. Not with Charleston. One other question. Who besides you drove wolf hunters out?"

"Just Frank Fournier. Francis Fournier. He's the only one I know. But he wouldn't run and hide, no more'n we would. You can ask him."

"I will," I said and went out.

Charleston heard my report without interruption. When I ended, he said, "We can check on Jordan's poker players, but I doubt it's worth it. Maybe later. And who knows about those wolf hunters? They could dummy up so as to protect one of the party. I doubt that, too. The truck was right there plain to see, even in the dark."

"I have to talk to Fournier later. He usually comes into town after supper."

Charleston gave a slow nod. "By the way, Pete Howard called. He was relieved. That dead cow of ours isn't his baby."

"It's ours then," I said needlessly. "I don't know, but it seems to me we've kind of lost sight of Pudge Eaton's death. Tim Reagan mentioned that. He asked were the two killings connected."

Charleston put a hand to his forehead, then to his cheeks. It didn't altogether erase the lines of worry and of fatigue. He had taken the late shift last night and, I suspected, gone on until daylight. I knew from the switchboard report that he had answered four calls, all unimportant but all in the line of duty. "Jase," he said, "I thought I was beginning to see a pattern. I thought I was fitting some pieces together. Now I don't know. Now I wonder."

He was still wondering when I took off.

◆◆◆ 20 ◆◆◆

OVER A FRIED-CHICKEN DINNER, which the pup wanted to share, Mother said, "I've changed his name."

"To what?"

"Bipsie seemed a sort of namby-pamby, little-girl's name, inappropriate for a male dog."

"So, Mother?"

"I debated between Leo and Rex."

"Lion or king, huh?"

"I decided on Rex. He's coming to know it. I declare, Jase, I never realized what company a dog could be."

"You become dependent on his dependence, like old Mr. Linderman. The king and his subject?"

"Now don't get fancy with me, Son. You always want to frazzle things out." She smiled forgivingly.

After dinner, putting first things first, I went to see Felix Underwood. He came to the door himself, invited me in and said his wife had gone to play cards. He led me into his den, across the new carpet that, by lamplight at least, didn't show where Doolittle had watered it.

The den consisted of a desk, a swivel chair, a straight chair and walls plastered with prints of baseball players. The oldest one I saw went back to Ty Cobb. On the desk was a picture of Willie Mays, which Underwood explained he was tardy in putting up. He had few interests beyond live balls and dead bodies, and of the two the former came first.

After we were seated, I said, "I came to make arrangements for Chuck Cleaver's funeral."

"All right, Jase boy. Wasn't that the damndest thing?"

I agreed that it was and added, "Mrs. Cleaver wants the funeral to be at two o'clock tomorrow afternoon, graveside services."

Underwood's plump face could wear three expressions — jovial, serious and funereal — which turned on and off according to circumstances. Now was the time for serious. "What! A grave's got to be dug. That's too short notice." He wanted me to think that digging a grave was all hand work, but I knew better.

"A closed casket, too. No viewing."

"Are you crazy, Jase? Or is she?"

"That's the way she wants it."

"After all the work I did on him. I tell you he was a challenge, and I met it. He makes a comely corpse now, and no one to appreciate the pains I took." His expression turned to funereal.

"That's not all, Felix. She hasn't much ready money. That's what she told me, and I believe her. So go easy on the coffin."

This was business and called for the serious look. "A rough pine box, huh, held together by shingle nails? She doesn't want him put away proper?"

"I'd say in the neighborhood of four hundred dollars. No more."

He heaved the sigh of the defeated. "Every day people are killing me."

"Killing each other is more on the mark."

"That's not to say I like it. What else?"

"I told her you would send a car out to the ranch to get her and take her back."

"That's part of our service, but you're damn free with your promises. Look, Jase, don't let this officer business go to your head. It's done enough already. You used to be a baseball pitcher with a good arm and one hell of a lot of promise. Then what? You got your hand banged up playing cop."

"That was a good time ago, and the hand's healed, but I've changed ambitions."

"Sandy Koufax for J. Edgar Hoover. That's what I call comin' down."

"That's spilt milk, Felix. Now about the funeral, there's one other thing. You got a preacher on tap?"

"Oh, sure. They come out of a spigot. Pull the handle, that's all, and here's one clerical — dressed with a Bible in his hands."

"All right. Can you engage a minister?"

"That costs, too. Preachers got to live just like you and I."

"Isn't the fee included in your services?"

Instead of answering, he asked, "What denomination?"

"I would say a preacher, not a priest."

"Cases like this, I usually go Methodist or Lutheran."

"Good enough. Mrs. Cleaver isn't particular."

"She sure isn't," he said, probably thinking of the cheap casket. He got up, turning jovial now that our business was done. "I'll take care of things, Jase. Just leave it to your old Uncle Felix." He patted my shoulder as I took my leave.

On the way to the Bar Star I stopped off at the public telephone booth and called Anita. Same story. Grandfather maybe a little bit better but needing almost constant attention. Not a good time for me to come calling.

Francis Fournier was in the saloon, along with eight or ten others. When I had cut him out of the bunch and said I wanted to talk to him, he said, "This is no good place for talk. A quiet coffee, huh?" He had a swarthy skin and a desperado's mustache at odds with his fundamental good humor.

We crossed the street to the Commercial Cafe, which wasn't busy at this hour, and sat at a table. After we had ordered and been served coffee, I said, "It's about the shooting of Chuck Cleaver."

"Sure. I guessed so. A bad thing, that."

"Mr. Charleston thinks one of you wolf hunters could have shot him by accident."

"Not so."

"What's not so?"

"Mr. Charleston, he is a smart man. He don't think that."

"He said it was a possibility."

"I heard him. You know so. A good trick, that's what he played. I take my hat off." Speaking, he tipped his old hat.

"Trick?" I asked.

"We were hot in the head. All of us. Me, too. There in the Bar Star. A fool thing we thought we do, to scare off the strip miners. Guilty? Not guilty? Who knows?"

He took a drink of coffee and wiped his mustache with a knuckle. "So we voted for a war party. Then comes your smart sheriff and says maybe a wolf hunter shot Cleaver. Them who hadn't hunted thought maybe so. He gave them to think. Us, too, us hot-heads. The party fizzled out. I said it was a smart trick."

"That's your way of looking at it," I said. "But what with whiskey and all, one of you could have shot Cleaver."

"And kept a tight mouth? No, Beard. We are better men than that. Charleston knows."

"You did some wild shooting."

"Fun shooting. I went for that. Not to kill anything."

"Not even wolves?"

He grinned, drank and spread his hands. "Wolves. They are big brothers to coyotes, not standing around to be shot. Too smart for that. They howl, but a man comes or a headlight, and they are the hell gone."

"Then why go hunting the way you did?"

"They did not know as much as me about wolves, and I was not telling. Let them hunt, have a good time."

We had finished with coffee. "You don't leave me anything to go on," I said. "In my place where would you look?"

He didn't answer at once. Then he told me, "Look down a gopher hole."

At first I thought he was joking. Then I suspected he wasn't. He was only half Indian, if that, but for an instant I saw him seated at a council fire minus his mustache, his appearance all Indian, his hair in plaits, his hand holding a pipe. It was a time for grave thought.

I said, "The gophers aren't out yet."

"One was."

I shook the mystical business out of my head. "Before I peek down gopher holes, I have to question the other hunters."

"Waste your time, huh?"

"Maybe so, but can you give me names?"

"Of everybody, I think," he answered, nodding. "For myself and for Bodie Dunn."

Without hesitation he told me names, and I jotted them

down. As we left the place, after I'd thanked him, he said, "The sheriff, he will find the hole. He is smart."

Before it was too late to ring doorbells, I had time to question two of the hunters he had named. They were no help.

I started walking home in the dark, thinking of the long chore of talking to everyone who had gone looking for wolves. A long chore and probably fruitless but more to the point than peering down burrows. The chinook wind still blew, warm and gentle as a remembered caress. Then there was the sound of torn air behind me, and before I could turn a massed weight hit me in the back and knocked me flat, face down. I got my hands under me and started to lift myself, and a great, slobbering tongue washed my neck. I knew then.

I said, "Damn you, Gunnar, quit it! Get away! Think you're the Hound of the Baskervilles?"

He stood there, tongue out, tail wagging, as I got to my feet. Friends deserved a pat on the head. I gave him a couple.

❖❖❖ 21 ❖❖❖

I ATTENDED CLEAVER's funeral as a matter of courtesy on the part of the sheriff's office. I didn't expect to see the culprit there, no matter the belief that the guilty out of some perversity liked to see their victims put safely away. I scanned the crowd, just on the chance, but didn't get a clue.

Fifty or more people attended, though notice of the services was too late or too early for the weekly newspaper. News in our country had a habit of getting around without benefit of the press.

The minister read from the Bible, mostly Psalms, and referred to the assurance that our Father's house had many mansions. I never knew what that meant, and neither did the preacher, but it sounded impressive. I imagined that the mansion Cleaver would have wanted was a going ranch. Turning from promise to fact, the minister gave us vital statistics. I learned that Cleaver was born in Minnesota, came to Montana as a young man and was fifty years old when he died. Mrs. Cleaver sat in the mourner's car, courtesy of Felix Underwood. If she was mourning, I couldn't tell. From what I could see of it, I gathered that her dress or suit was deep purple. That color was mourning enough in itself.

Felix might dicker and wail, but he liked his funerals nice, and so he had recruited four middle-aged ladies, or older, who sang "The Old Rugged Cross." Their voices rose frail in the breeze, dying in the plains grass and among the tombstones. The old rugged cross, trembling and falling, weak but courageous, there on the hillside of the dead. I wanted to applaud the old girls for this quavering assertion of hope against everyone's destiny.

Right after the services I said to Sheriff Charleston, "I've interviewed six of the ten men who went hunting. Nothing there. Not a glimmer. Four to go, and I'll do it, but I won't get anything."

Seated behind his desk, he listened with what seemed impatience, as if obliged to hear me out. Then he said with uncommon brusqueness, "We're just festering. Chasing our tails. Marching up the hill and down again. Running fast in the same spot."

"Yes, sir," I answered, trying to lighten his mood. "I get the idea through the mixed metaphors."

He didn't smile. He said, "Any damn thing is better than fester. Let's have a drink or a beer and let the world wag."

"If you say so. Where?"

"The Chicken Shack. That suits the mood, and a friendly visit won't hurt us."

We climbed into his Special. On arrival, with the engine turned off, we could hear the juke box inside the place. When we entered, the sound stunned us. For a minute we stood by the door, letting our ears deaden while we looked around. A half-dozen customers, not known to me by name, were working on drinks at bar or table. Ves Eaton was behind the counter. I shouted for a whiskey and a beer. Eaton seemed friendly enough. The customers appeared curious, not hostile. I took the drinks to a table, and Charleston and I endured the racket.

Presently the music came to an end, and humans could communicate without lip-reading. His glass of whiskey half-raised, Charleston shook his head slowly and said, "Who said the world ends with a whimper? It ends with a blast, jungle drums beating, jungle voices crying out bloody murder."

"Yes, sir," I answered. "If this place wasn't walled in, the courthouse could dance to hard rock."

Another record came on, and our talk went off.

Charleston was about to take a sip of the whiskey when a look came on his face. Later I was to call it a look of wonder, then recognition. He got up, his glass barely touched. His lips said, "Come on!"

We climbed back in the Special. Once we were rolling, I said, "May I ask where to?"

"To get Cleaver's truck."

I didn't understand but didn't push, respecting Charleston's mood, which appeared to shy off from talk.

So we wheeled along, silent, over the new-breathing land where, I thought, life was stirring under the warming soil, where gophers would appear before long and the carpet flowers bloom.

Just once did he speak again while the Special moved along. That was to say, "Dry year this year. Hard on the farmers."

"Plenty of time for snow yet," I answered.

He didn't reply, having dismissed the subject already. We passed the mourner's car, minus the mourner, bound back for town.

Three cars were parked by the Cleaver house. Inside were old Mr. and Mrs. Whitney, Ernest Linderman, Judge and Mrs.

Church, and the widow, who let us in without comment other than a hello. On the table were a couple of casseroles, a baked turkey, two loaves of bread, a cake and a pie, plus extras. After we had greeted the company, Mrs. Cleaver, as if yielding to the demands of the occasion, said, "Even with a sick grandpa, that nice Anita Dutton found time to bake a cake. Omar Test brought it over. Want something to eat?"

I felt Charleston's eyes on me and heard him say, "I believe we have time to sample Miss Dutton's cake."

It was good cake, sweet and moist as I liked it.

We chatted a little while we munched. I had noticed before that post-burial parties appeared perky and light of heart, and I wondered again if that were to bolster the bereft or to celebrate survival. A man is dead: long live us.

Charleston maneuvered Mrs. Cleaver aside. "I wonder if we could borrow your truck for a day or two, Mrs. Cleaver?" he asked. "I hate to suggest it at this time, but it might help us in our investigation."

She answered, "I ain't going anywhere," and took keys from a hook on a cupboard.

We went outside and looked at the truck. There was nothing in the bed but the big toolbox, a large plastic sack, empty, and four short fence posts. I was about to remove all but the fixed-in-place toolbox when Charleston shook his head. Then he asked, "Mind driving it?" I didn't.

"Park it in one of our slots," he told me.

So, rattling along after him, I drove the truck in, asking myself the meaning, the significance, the why of this old bundle of bolts. Cleaver couldn't have been shot from inside it, not if we were to credit the evidence. Neither could the thing speak.

Charleston was waiting when I parked the truck. Before I

could get out, he climbed into the passenger's seat. He studied the dash and began nodding his head. He asked, "Know anything about tape decks?"

"Very little," I answered and was exaggerating at that. I must have been the only young man and one of the few of any age who knew almost nothing about tapes and sound gadgets. I could take music or leave it alone. Tin ear, classmates had said.

"No load in this thing," Charleston said, pointing to a slot. "Run to the drugstore. Get a tape, eight track."

"Yes, sir."

I trotted to the store, a block and a half away. The clerk, a new girl, must have thought I was crazy, buying any old eight-track tape and rushing off with it. Three or four dogs were sniffing around the truck.

Charleston took a quick look at the tape before inserting it. "The saints go marching in," he said and touched a button.

My head blew off.

I had listened to juke boxes turned on full blast. In crowded bars I had been afflicted with the caterwauling of singers and the exaggerated tones of guitars. I had followed close to brass bands tooting and thumping out Sousa. They didn't compare.

I jumped out of the truck, which was shaking in all its tin timbers. The saints kept marching in while heads popped out of courthouse windows and passing bodies were arrested in full flight.

Charleston turned off the sound and got out. He mounted the truck bed and went to the toolbox. Two self-locking latches secured it. He worked at them, then said to me, "Get a screwdriver from the Special." With it he wrenched off the latches. The box opened from the front, not the top. Two speakers crowded the box; I didn't see any tools. Charleston let himself down. Tad Frazier had appeared from the office. Charleston told him, "Watch it. No tinkering."

Charleston led the way, shooing off dogs and explaining to the small crowd that had gathered around, "Testing. Just testing." Like saints, we marched into his office.

Seated, he said as an aside, "It would have been even louder with the box open."

"I can hardly hear you."

"Head ringing, huh?"

"If it's still there."

He raised his voice. "One mystery solved. Get it?"

I answered, "Glimmers."

"Cleaver knew his electronics," he went on, veering away from what I wanted to hear. "I don't understand the mechanics myself, but he wired the thing up, leaving no open sign, and he's sure to have put in a booster. That accounts for the volume."

"Yes, sir."

"Cleaver may have got his idea somewhere else. That notion occurs to me."

"Where else?"

"From a book."

I just looked at him, and he went on. "You didn't notice the books in Cleaver's house? No. Well, two of them were by a man named Jim Corbett. He hunted man-eating tigers in India. I read those books years ago."

I said, "Yes?"

"I dug one story out of my memory. It told that one man-eating tiger, just one, kept thousands of construction workers cowering in camp, afraid to go out on the job. Cleaver might have gone on from there."

"With wolves, huh?"

"If one tiger could intimidate thousands, a pack of wolves ought to scare off a few."

"It almost did."

"We'll never prove the connection, though the theory makes sense. And Cleaver had another thing going for him. Mutilated animals. People were, are, still spooky about them."

"But one man couldn't unload a full-grown steer unless he had a dump truck."

"He could if he placed it on rollers. That's what those bob-tailed fence posts were for. Cleaver stole behind the row camps at night, no lights, and just rolled off the carcass. No sweat except the fear of being seen." He paused while I nodded and then resumed. "He worked to make the steer look as if it had been mutilated by wolves. The miners were quick to think it had been. Some probably do yet. But there was a flaw that trained men could see. The steer was his own, and he had to cut off and scratch off the rib band. Wolves wouldn't have gnawed there, not while better bites were available."

"I see, but what about that gang of dogs — wolves to the miners — that gathered in the alley?"

"There's an answer to that, too, I think. Suppose Cleaver's old bitch dog came in heat. Suppose he put her in a plastic sack so as to confine the scent, took her to the alley at night and walked her up and down while she left her sign. Then back into the bag and away. You saw the sack. You noticed just now that the open sack was attracting dogs. To keep in the scent, Cleaver had tied it at his dog's neck while transporting her. There's a piece of cord in the truck you might not have noticed."

So he had answers to everything, I thought, feeling a long shot less than bright. Answers to everything but two things, so I asked, "What about shooting up the Chicken Shack? What about killing Pudge Eaton? That's off the mark."

Charleston nodded his head. "You're right there. We'll probably never have proof that Cleaver did the shooting. But look at it this way. From the evidence we have we know how fixed in purpose he was. Suppose, then, that the shooting was a first effort. Perhaps he thought at the time that the shooting would be enough. Suppose he hadn't hit on the idea of borrowing from Jim Corbett. Of course he didn't mean to hit Eaton, and, if he did kill him, that fact must have come as a shock. Men react differently to the knowledge of guilt. Having killed a man, Cleaver may have become all the more determined to carry on. A crime committed often frees onward forces. It points the course. Proof or not, I'm satisfied that was the way it was."

One question remained. "So how was it that Mr. Willsie's window got broken?"

He was a long time in answering and after a silence didn't answer at all. "I'm fiddling around in my mind, Jase," he said, and fiddled some more. At last he asked, "Cleaver had a reputation for honesty. Right?"

"Some people thought he was slow in his mind, but everybody said he was honest down to the quick."

"An honest man, then. He couldn't do anything to square up with Pudge Eaton. But Willsie? Maybe I have the ghost of a hunch."

He turned to the telephone, got an outside line and presently said, "Chick Charleston here, Mr. Willsie. How are you? Yes, fine. Thanks. I'm wondering if anyone ever came forward to pay for your broken window. No? I see. Good-bye, then."

To me he said, "Just a chance, Jase, and hardly that. We

never inspected Cleaver's truck, except for the toolbox and the bed. Go waste some time on it, will you?"

I took the ignition key and went to the truck. The key didn't fit the glove compartment, but a screwdriver sprang the lid. There was nothing important inside. I dismounted and moved the seat and there it was, a wrinkled envelope that bore the name in block letters, MR. LEONARD WILLSIE. I took it to Charleston without opening it.

His eyes lit up when he saw it. He slit the seal. Inside were two fifty-dollar bills. "The long shot paid off," he said. "Cleaver broke Willsie's window so as to involve the strip miners, but he was going to pay Willsie for it. How to get the money to him, that was the question."

For a full moment Charleston was silent. His tone was musing when he spoke again. "Cleaver was a better man than anyone thought, far more intelligent than we gave him credit for. And was he set on preserving his ranch! I wonder what would have been his next move. I wonder what he would have done, given time for his second wind."

He rose and took a slow turn around his chair. "He had people believing in wolves because they heard wolves. Six miles they carry on a still Arctic night, so Doolittle says. How far on a tape amplified? What's more, he had actually shot a wolf, probably a single stray from the north. He could, and I bet did, tell about it and show the pelt to the doubtful. Strong evidence. Some schemer, that Cleaver. I salute him."

It was back to business when he sat down again. "Who shot Cleaver? That's next. Find the wolf tape, and you find the killer."

He said "you," I thought. He meant me. He still wanted me to believe the case was my own.

❖❖❖ 22 ❖❖❖

I HAD BEEN TOLD to make my own hours, and I was making them the following night when Charleston rang the bell. Mother went to the door and, pleased to see him, invited him in. Bipsie — no, Rex — made a friendly fuss. Nothing would do then but that Mother go to the kitchen, bring in a piece of pie and a cup of coffee and hand them to him. We exchanged some meaningless small talk.

When Charleston had finished his pie, he turned to me. "Nothing new at my end of the line," he said.

I spoke a little defensively, not having visited the office all day. "I chased down the last of the wolf hunters and took their statements. No help."

"I'm not surprised," he answered. "It was a long shot."

Mother got up, took his plate and cup and said, "Please excuse me, you two. I have things to do in the kitchen."

She didn't. She just thought it fit to absent herself and let the men talk.

Charleston took a thin cigar from his pocket and lit up. I

pushed an ashtray closer to him. After a puff or two he said, "Let's recap, Jase."

"The whole case?"

"Start with Cleaver out alone with his truck. Put yourself in his place. Use his methods."

"All right, but I don't see much point to it, Mr. Charleston."

"There probably isn't any, but it can't hurt. Go ahead."

"It must have been this way: Cleaver drove out and parked his truck here and there, according to what little breeze there was. He wanted the sound to carry into the town. Then he opened the toolbox and turned on the wolves."

"Yes."

"If he saw car lights coming his way, he turned off the recorder, slammed shut the toolbox, took his rifle and walked away from the truck. He could say he was hunting wolves, too."

"The man who shot him sneaked up on foot? That's what you think?"

"A car without lights might have come pretty close, but I doubt it."

"So do I," Charleston said. "Was the sound still turned on when he was shot?"

"I guess so. Does it matter?"

Charleston ignored the question. "Say a man sneaked up on foot. Who was he, and why did he fire?"

"Some enemy, I suppose."

"An enemy, or someone annoyed by the hoax? Someone deeply resentful?"

"Who could be that annoyed?"

Charleston put a match to his dead cigar. "A scared man. A man whose wife had been scared. Whose kids had. Does that hold water?"

"Not much to me," I replied. "If he had caught on to Cleaver, why not just expose him?"

"Good question. But there's no telling what a man badly scared will do when he finds he's been made a fool of. Maybe the killer wanted to confront Cleaver. Maybe they got into a quarrel. That's possible."

"A long time ago you told me anything's possible. But it's a big order, talking to everyone who might have been spooked. Anyhow, they wouldn't admit it. What's the use?"

Charleston smiled after he had blown out a plume of smoke. "I'm just bouncing ideas around for whatever benefit they may be to you. Don't be upset."

"I'm offended because I'm not getting anywhere. I'm offended because I don't know which way to turn. I'm a wonderful deputy."

"Just as I'm a wonderful sheriff, being as much at a loss as you are. Another nagger, Jase. Why did the killer steal the tape?"

"If he did steal it."

"If he did. All we know is that it's missing. All we know is that it wasn't on Cleaver's body. All we know is that it didn't jump out and run. So it must have been stolen. That leaves the big why."

"Keepsake?"

"Maybe. A damn dangerous one."

"I think of some maybe crazy things."

"Like what?"

"We have one man dead on each side. That's how feuds start, isn't it?"

"Unlikely," he answered. "Feuds are family affairs. They're personal. The cause is forgotten, mired down in family hate. Dead end there, I think."

"Maybe I ought to find out where Cleaver got the tape?"

"I don't see how that could help us."

Charleston rose from his chair. "All right for now, Jase. I doubt we've made any progress."

It turned out we hadn't. Charleston had hoped, I gathered, for some fresh idea through the rehash of the case. Dead end again.

An uneventful day passed and part of another. Uneventful in a sense. Hysteria doesn't die overnight. Old fears linger in spite of proof and assurances. So foolish calls kept coming in. We answered some of them and found Labradors, setters, German shepherds and one toy terrier. No wolves.

I wasn't getting anywhere, and a feeling of urgency, combined with defeat, built up in me. Charleston didn't question me. He didn't push. But I sensed his impatience, not with me alone but with himself, the whole staff and continuing bafflement. On foot and by car I roamed the streets and the countryside, thinking, looking, asking questions — and standing still. When asked about progress what could we say? Just that we're stumped?

I went back on shift — which meant I was seldom off it. Hours put in didn't count. My salary was a gift, unearned.

It didn't help that the fun had gone out of Doolittle. Not only the fun but the sense of companionship. In his quiet and uncommon presence, I felt depressed. It didn't help that Anita kept putting me off, pleading her grandfather's illness.

I talked to Charleston about Doolittle. "Have I hurt his feelings somehow? Have I offended him?" I asked. "To me, maybe only to me, he's a different Ike."

"Let it ride, Jase," Charleston answered. "It's not your fault. It may be some trouble of his own. People have a habit of visiting their moods on others. I wouldn't pay undue attention."

But what was undue attention? What would come out in the eventual wash, if anything? How keep a friendship when you felt the friendship was breaking? By distance? By unconcern? Those tactics wouldn't work. I couldn't accept them.

On the afternoon of the second day I cornered Doolittle alone in the sheriff's office. In his hand was a paper cup of office coffee. "It's brewed fresh," he said. "Get yourself some. I have to be going."

"You don't have to go anywhere, and you know it. I want to talk to you, Ike."

"Talk away."

"Something's eating on you. What is it?"

"If there is, it will pass." He wouldn't look at me. He looked at the cup in his hand.

"If I can help — "

"Who needs help?"

"Damn it, Ike, you do! That's who. Or maybe it's me. What have I done to make you so offish? I thought we were friends."

"Sure we're friends, Jase. Always will be, I hope."

"You don't act friendly."

"Sorry." He took a mouthful of coffee and chewed it as if he had never tasted coffee before. "Things been on my mind."

"What things?"

"If you have to know, I'm quitting this job."

"The hell you are!" My words held unbelief. They burst out of me.

"I'm not cut out for it."

"You're a damn good deputy."

"Sure. Sportin' my badge around. Talkin' big. Actin' big.

Throwin' my weight. Showin' up with a shotgun all the same like Bat Masterson."

"By showing up with it you gave Charleston the time he needed to calm down that mob."

"He would have made out without me. Hell, I know that. Me, the small-size showboat."

"Your reasons aren't good enough. Not for me. What, for a fact, goes with you, Ike?"

"Nothin' except show off."

"You know I'll help if I can."

"Resignations don't need any help. That's what I'm doing, right now."

"For God's sake why, Ike? Tell me the truth."

Now his eyes lifted to mine. "Just say in my time I've hurt enough people. This is a hurting job, Jase, if you do it right."

"It hurts more if you don't do it or do it wrong."

"Think so?" His words were more denial than question. His eyes were sad.

"I do think so. Let the chips fall. That sounds harsh, but it has to be that way in law enforcement."

He tossed the empty coffee cup in the wastebasket almost as if he were throwing something precious away. His eyes lifted again, still sad, and he was slow in responding. "Maybe so. Maybe so. And bein' so hell-bent on the law, you don't hesitate about hurt. Let the chips fall, and even if they injure somebody that's the way it is. I'm not built like that, Jase." He wasn't arguing. He was asking, even pleading.

"I'm not unfeeling, Ike, but when you're a deputy — and you're a good one — you have to do a deputy's job."

He sounded a long sigh. The strength seemed to have seeped out of him, and the spirit. I had leaned on him, and damn me for doing it. "Don't rag me, Jase," he said. "Here it is, and it's all of it. Who misters everybody? Who misters you? Who misters me?"

When at last I understood, I said, "Good God! the telephone caller. The tip about Cleaver's death. Not him, Ike! Not him!"

Doolittle was on his way to the door. "Concealing evidence. Add that to my list. I'm quitting."

I followed him out. He was asking Blanche Burton if she would type out what he said. I brushed on by, walked down the courthouse hall to the side door and let myself out, almost upsetting Charleston who was on the way in. He asked, "What's the rush, Jase?"

I pushed past him, saying, "Got to look down a gopher hole." Then I called over my shoulder, "Don't let Doolittle resign."

I knew his questioning eyes were on me as I walked to an officer car. A fine, respectful deputy I was, being brusque to my superior, to a man who had shown me nothing but kindness. Yeah, ever so grateful.

The road to the Dutton place was long and wearisome. I closed my mind to all but the trip, though Anita kept slipping in. At least I would see her again.

Omar Test was in a corral next to the barn, some distance away from the house. I pulled up there. In the corral with Omar was a cow and a calf that stood unsteady on legs just discovered and nuzzled at the cow's flank. I stepped down from the car. The warm wind from the west had died, succeeded by a chill northern breeze. Omar had seen me. He said, grinning, "Early calf, Mr. Beard, but ain't he a dandy?"

"Can you leave him and come to the car, out of the wind?"

"Sure thing." He came through a gate and took a seat beside me.

"Chuck Cleaver's death," I said. "Let's talk about it."

"That was a shame. He wasn't a bad man far as I know."

"Someone didn't agree."

"It was an accident."

"How do you know?"

"That's just what I figger. Couldn't be anything else, could it?"

"Keep talking."

"What's there to say, Mr. Beard?"

"All that you know."

Test edged away from me. "No, sir, Mr. Beard. I couldn't do that."

"We have evidence that points to you."

"Points how?"

"As the one who killed Cleaver."

A look of slow comprehension came into his face. He might not have heard me say he was entitled to an attorney. His voice came out muted. "Me? I never shot a man in my whole life, just like I never took a drink. You know that, Mr. Beard."

"I'm sure you never took a drink. That's all."

He put his big hands to his face. "I don't want to talk no more. Please, Mr. Beard."

"It's not enough to say you didn't shoot Cleaver."

"But I never. I tell you I never." One hand made a little gesture, indicating the end of the world.

I asked, "Who did then?"

"They been so good to me. All along they been so good." The big cipher of a man wiped at his eyes, missing a tear.

Words didn't come to me, not at once. They pushed up, half-formed, to my mouth and stayed there. Mine was a hurting job and the hell with it, but there was the law. The truth had to come out. Let the hurtful chips fall.

Omar said, "It ain't fair, Mr. Beard. It ain't right."

"Neither is killing a man."

"He didn't know what he was doing. He ain't to blame being what he is in the head. Can't you forget it?"

"Go on, Omar."

"Miss Anita, she takes peeks into his room, see if he's all right. He wasn't in his bed, so she come to me."

"I see," I said, not wanting to.

"He's awful spry for an old man, but it was too much for him. I found him. He was halfway to comin' back. Then he tuckered out and just lay down in the cold. I packed him home. He took sick then."

"Then you went back?"

"Yes, sir. When I found him, I could make out a truck farther on. So I tromped out there, and you know what I found."

"Did he have a rifle with him?"

"Yes, sir, he did."

"I thought that rifle was hidden."

"Way he pokes around, nothin' stays hid very long."

"Why would he want to shoot Cleaver?"

"That's where you're wrong. Mr. Beard. He didn't want to. He mistook him for a wolf. He couldn't see good at all."

I knew he couldn't.

I asked, "Did he have a little box with him, like you get music from?"

"A tape, they call it. He had it tight in his hand."

"Why would he take that?"

Omar had quit crying now that the worst was said, but his expression was mournful. "Hard tellin', Mr. Beard. I savvy old folks pretty good. They got notions like kids, not so smart, though. He would take and hide things and forget where they were, like my jackknife once and Miss Anita's necklace. And he liked noise. Got a cassette of his own, and he turned it up till the shingles shook until she made him lower it."

"She has the tape?"

"She cached it away somewhere."

I drew a deep breath and said, "Thanks, Omar. You've been a big help." He didn't believe me. Neither did I.

"I swore to keep mum," he said mournfully. "I couldn't put no blame on her if she gave me my time."

"She won't fire you. Now stick around, Omar. We'll want your statement. I'll drive you to town and bring you back. I must talk to Miss Anita."

We both got out of the car. Omar returned to the corral. My legs were old. The calf acted frisky. I pointed myself in the direction of the house and made my legs take me.

Anita answered the door, saying, "Yes?" and no more. Her face held not even a trace of a remembered smile.

I took off my hat and said, "Anita, I'm sorry. I've been talking to Omar."

"You mean you made him talk."

"I suppose you could say that. I had to, Anita." I couldn't bring assurance into my voice.

"I know," she answered. "You kill weeds." Her small jaw was square. I could see muscles rippling at the hinge. She spoke with a tight mouth.

"It's my job, Anita. Please understand. And I'm just as sorry as can be."

"Sure. Your job. And you'll take a sick old man in and jail him and try him and put him behind bars, when he doesn't know what it's all about. You know what you can do with your job, Mr. Beard."

"Now, no such thing," I said, my voice rising in protest. "It won't be like that. I'm not taking him in. If he has to go to town, it will be by ambulance when he is well again. And he won't be tried. He'll be put in good custodial care."

"Now shall we all recite the Lord's Prayer?"

I said, "It would make things easier for you." It was a stupid remark.

If ever I saw contempt on a face, it came on hers. "Thanks for relieving me of a great inconvenience."

In the jumble of my thoughts it occurred to me to ask how Grandfather was.

"Just fine and dandy," she replied. "He can't wait for that good custodial care."

I said, "Anita, Anita," and my voice trailed off. All I could say then was, "Do you have the tape?"

She left without speaking, left me at the door without inviting me in. She returned and handed me the tape and said, "Good-bye, Mr. Beard," and closed the door.

I rounded up Omar and headed for town.

❖❖❖ 23 ❖❖❖

"WHEN THE SPRING QUARTER STARTS, I'm going back to school," I told Charleston.

We were alone in the office. It was late afternoon, but the days had lengthened, and a long sunbeam shone through one window and found some dust particles. It was misleading, for a north wind was blowing outside.

"As long as I'm in office, you can always have a job here, now, later, whenever," Charleston answered.

I mumbled my thanks. We both went silent, each with his own thoughts. Charleston fingered the tape I had brought in, fingered it idly, not looking at it. I knew its label.

Voices of the Wild

WOLVES

Omar Test had made his statement the day before. It jibed with what he had told me. A dismal business, listening to him again, but I had to be there to prompt him. Afterwards Tad Frazier had driven him back to the Dutton ranch, kindness of Charleston, who seemed to know I didn't want to. The case against Mr. Dutton could wait.

Now I said, "I'm glad Doolittle decided to stay on."

"I told him if he didn't I'd charge him with obstructing justice. He knew I was joshing but still came around."

I wanted to get away from myself, so I said, "Tim Reagan would make a good deputy."

"Not so quick with the suggestions, Jase. Your mind is made up about school?"

It was. I thought of kind people trying to spare others — Ike Doolittle, trying to protect me and Anita; Omar Test doing his best to fence off Anita and Grandpa; Anita keeping mum for the sake of the old man. And here I had come in the name of the law and torn that shielding away. To what end? To expose a dotty old gaffer as harmless now as a cradled baby. I had acted as a good officer should, as the law expected. Damn the law, and yet, and yet.

"I'm stale on the job, Mr. Charleston. I need a change."

"Stale, is it, Jase? After good work?"

It went against what I'd planned to say, but I said, "I feel kind of down, Mr. Charleston."

"I know, Jase. I know, boy," he said slowly, with so much compassion in his voice, so much sympathy, that I dared not look at his face.

He went on. "Choices, Jase. Choices. They come so damn hard, but a man has to make them, knowing or not knowing they'll be trailed by regrets. I'm sorry, Jase. By God I'm sorry."

I heard him straighten in his chair. His tone changed. "All right. Do what seems best. Quit when it's convenient. But you're not resigning. I'm giving you a leave of absence."

I hardly had time to thank him before he was buzzed by the switchboard. The words came over. "A man to see you, Mr. Charleston."

Charleston looked at me, and I nodded to indicate our conversation was done. "Send him in," he said.

There entered one Kingston Tuttle, alias Henry David Thoreau. He was as thin as a string of jerky. His jacket hung loose. He had tucks in his pants. He advanced and stuck out his hand. "Remember me?" he asked in a voice rusty from disuse. "I'm the guy who shot himself in the foot and lied about it."

Charleston said, "We remember. Turned over a new leaf, huh?"

"Leaves. Thoreau's leaves. He wouldn't have lied. I came to apologize and thank you for your help."

"I will be damned!" Charleston said.

"I kept reading him and reading him and feeling guiltier with every word."

"You stayed in your camp? How'd you make out?"

"Yeah, I stayed and made out pretty good. But Thoreau had an edge on me. There were fish in Walden Pond and he caught them and ate them. So, next time around, we'll be even up."

"Guess how, Jase," Charleston said.

I didn't feel like guessing.

"You tell me then, Tuttle."

"I'll fish in the summer and smoke what I catch."

"You'll actually try it again?"

"I will. A man deserves another chance. I'm just getting my second wind."

"Good luck," Charleston said and looked at his watch. "Past supper time. My wife's gone to the big town to shop. How about a square meal on me?"

Tuttle burst out, "Oh, boy!"

"Jase?"

I knew Charleston aimed to divert me, but I begged off, saying my mother would have dinner ready.

I walked in the chill wind and entered the Bar Star. Besides Bob Studebaker behind the bar only one man was there. He was Tony Coletti. I bought him a drink and drank with him — too much. Studebaker went from behind the bar, peeked through a front window and announced it was snowing outside.